WITHDRAWN
Winnetka-Northfield Public Library
W9-AOK-132
AUG - - 2023
WINNETKA-NORTHFIELD
PUBLIC LIBRARY DISTRICT
WINNETKA, IL 60093
847-446-7220

BY NINA GEORGE

The Little Village of Book Lovers

The Book of Dreams

The Little French Bistro

The Little Paris Bookshop

The
Little Village
of
Book Lovers

The Little Village *of* Book Lovers

A NOVEL

Nina George

BALLANTINE BOOKS
NEW YORK

The Little Village of Book Lovers is a work of fiction. Names, characters, places, and incidents are the products of the author's imagination or are used fictitiously. Any resemblance to actual events, locales, or persons, living or dead, is entirely coincidental.

Translation copyright © 2023 by Simon Pare

All rights reserved.

Published in the United States by Ballantine Books, an imprint of Random House, a division of Penguin Random House LLC, New York.

Ballantine is a registered trademark and the colophon is a trademark of Penguin Random House LLC.

Originally published in Germany as *Südlichter* by Knaur Verlag, an imprint of Verlagsgruppe Droemer Knaur, Munich, Germany, in 2019.
Copyright © 2019 by Knaur Verlag.

This translation published in the United Kingdom by Michael Joseph, an imprint of Penguin Books Limited, a Penguin Random House Company.

LIBRARY OF CONGRESS CATALOGING-IN-PUBLICATION DATA
Names: George, Nina, author. | Pare, Simon, translator.
Title: The little village of book lovers: a novel / Nina George; [translated by Simon Pare].
Other titles: Südlichter. English
Description: New York: Ballantine Books, [2023]
Identifiers: LCCN 2022039685 (print) | LCCN 2022039686 (ebook) | ISBN 9780593157886 (hardcover; acid-free paper) | ISBN 9780593157893 (ebook)
Subjects: LCGFT: Romance fiction. | Novels.
Classification: LCC PT2707.E59 S8313 2023 (print) | LCC PT2707.E59 (ebook) | DDC 833/.92—dc23/eng/20220920
LC record available at https://lccn.loc.gov/2022039685
LC ebook record available at https://lccn.loc.gov/2022039686

PRINTED IN THE UNITED STATES OF AMERICA ON ACID-FREE PAPER

randomhousebooks.com

2 4 6 8 9 7 5 3 1

First U.S. Edition

Title-page art: Алексей Панчин / stock.adobe.com (bookshelf), Alexandr / stock.adobe.com (paper)
Olive branch art: veri13 / stock.adobe.com
Book image: LeitnerR / stock.adobe.com

To Jens

The
Little Village
of
Book Lovers

A PROLOGUE FROM

THE LITTLE PARIS BOOKSHOP

"What do *you* do when you can't go on, Monsieur Perdu?" Jordan asked wearily.

"Me? Nothing."

Next to nothing.

I take night walks through Paris until I'm tired. I clean Lulu's *engine, the hull and the windows, and I keep the boat ready to go, right down to the last screw, even though it hasn't gone anywhere in two decades.*

I read books—twenty at a time. Everywhere: on the toilet, in the kitchen, in cafés, on the metro. I do jigsaw puzzles that take up the whole floor, destroy them when I've finished and then start all over again. I feed stray cats. I arrange my groceries in alphabetical order. I sometimes take sleeping tablets. I take a dose of Rilke to wake up. I don't read any books in which women like——crop up. I gradually turn to stone. I carry on. The same every day. That's the only way I can survive. But other than that, no, I do nothing.

Perdu made a conscious effort. The boy had asked for help; he didn't want to know how Perdu was. So give it.

The bookseller fetched his treasure out of the small, old-fashioned safe behind the counter.

Sanary's *Southern Lights*.

The only book Sanary had written—under that name, at any rate. "Sanary"—after the erstwhile town of refuge for exiled writers, Sanary-sur-Mer on the south coast of Provence—was an impenetrable pseudonym.

His—or her—publisher, Duprés, was in an old people's home out on Île-de-France enduring Alzheimer's with good cheer. During Perdu's visits, the elderly Duprés had served him up a couple dozen versions of who Sanary was and how the manuscript had come into his possession.

So Monsieur Perdu kept on searching.

For two decades he had been analyzing the rhythms of the language, the choice of words, and the cadence of the sentences, comparing the style and the subject matter with other authors'. Perdu had narrowed it down to eleven possible names: seven women and four men.

He would have loved to thank one of them, for Sanary's *Southern Lights* was the only thing that pierced him without hurting. Reading *Southern Lights* was a homeopathic dose of happiness. It was the only balm that could ease Perdu's pain—a gentle, cold stream over the scorched earth of his soul.

It was not a novel in the conventional sense, but a short story about the various kinds of love, full of wonderful invented words and infused with enormous humanity. The melancholy with which it described an inability to live each day to the full, to take every day for what it really was, namely unique, unrepeatable, and precious; how that dolefulness resonated with him.

He handed Jordan his last copy.

"Read this. Three pages every morning before breakfast, lying down. It has to be the first thing you take in."

SOUTHERN LIGHTS

SANARY

Everything is connected, says Love.

I know, says Death.

That's terribly illogical, says Logic.

The olive tree has its own thoughts on the matter.

1

Love and the Maiden

Marie-Jeanne's cradle stood under a broad-canopied olive tree some people claimed was over eight hundred years old, something the tree would neither confirm nor deny (at its age, one did not comment on how old one was).

She was giggling at the silvery rustling of the leaves, which were smiling in the gentle Pontias breeze. The wind was a local phenomenon, a last taste of magic in a century seemingly shorn of it. It was the steady breath of the four mountains—Essaillon, Garde Grosse, Saint Jaume, and Vaux—that shielded the town of Nyons like sentinels. The mountains breathed out in the morning, filling the valley of the river Eygues with the scent of herbs and the cool air of upland nights, always at the same time of day for precisely half an hour, and inhaled again after sundown every evening. This cool stream of air seemed to rise in the calanques and salty bays of the distant sea. It brought with it fragrances of lavender and mint and drove the searing heat from the day.

From the large kitchen—the main living space in every *mazet* in the Drôme Provençale, a place for cooking, chatting, staying silent, being born, and waiting for the end to come—Aimée was able to keep an eye on her granddaughter's cradle as she shuttled back and forth between the wood-fired stove and the table.

Aimée placed sliced potatoes, black Tanche olives, eggplants, and fresh pink garlic in a well-worn fluted baking tin; drizzled the vegetables with silky, hay-green olive oil; and scooped chunks of the local *fromagerie*'s fresh goat cheese from a clay dish. Last, she rubbed some sprigs of lime-scented wild thyme she'd picked the previous evening between her fingers.

A pan of milk was cooling on the windowsill. It would soon be time. Marie-Jeanne was quite capable of making her feelings known if her grandmother was too slow getting lunch ready.

Every time Aimée turned her face toward her granddaughter, her thousand sharp wrinkles softened into a far younger complexion.

The proud old olive tree went on singing its chanson to the little girl under its boughs. It hummed the secret song of the cicadas—*your light makes me sing*. It tickled her nose and cheeks with a dappling of shadows and delighted in the tiny fingers clutching at the breeze and in the waves of gurgling, heartfelt laughter issuing from her tummy.

Marie-Jeanne and Aimée. Each meant the world to the other.

It was love.

I watched Aimée Claudel, whom I had last touched many years ago, but she couldn't see me. Everyone knows me, but none can see me. I'm that thing you call love.

I came to Marie-Jeanne's grandmother early in her life.

She was barely thirteen at the time. It was summertime then, too—the record-breaking summer of 1911. Life took place outdoors. For weeks on end, this bright land boiled under the sun. After laboring since before sunrise, people whiled away the evening hours in blissful idleness. That summer was sweet and redolent with the melodies and whisperings of the leaves of the olive trees. The grasshoppers chirped their silvery tunes. And oh, the soft fall of the figs at night! The whole summer was like a dazzling fever.

I placed my burden on so many people that summer. How heavily I was to weigh on them only a few years later.

Aimée fell in love with a boy who used to sing as he worked in her father's milking parlor. First he became a soldier; in the Great War he became a man. He didn't return for many years and when he did, his boyish nature had retreated deep inside him, along with all his songs and all his colorful cheer. The mountains were so silent, but the roaring inside him was so loud. As his wife, Aimée spent the rest of her life exhuming his buried soul. She sang soft lullabies to him in the night when he screamed, chased the dullness from his eyes with patience, and fed him hot onion soup in the evenings when he drank. In the quiet, endless winter nights she warmed her husband's body with her bare skin to calm his incessant shivering. Her skin became softer and softer over the years, ever thinner, even as it burst with emotions and energy and cares. With life itself.

Back in the summer of 1911 I touched Aimée's skin, running my hands down her body from top to toe. She was naked and had just bathed in the Eygues's shimmering turquoise waters as they flowed toward the calm and mighty Rhône. She was beautiful, her straight back a symbol of her personality and fortitude, and she had a stout, tightly coiled soul. I poured a great deal of myself into her, maybe too much. Maybe I was in love with her—lovers pay no heed to how much they give, which is usually more than is desired. This was partly why I returned to see her, on the day the events you are going to hear about took place.

Aimée spent her whole life rescuing the lost boy inside the man. Every single day. I'd given her such an enormous capacity for love, and this capacity stirred the defiance and kindness in her nature that made her the woman she was.

When the second war began to rage, it came to Nyons too. Yes, it hurts, the memory of boots ringing out on the cobbles and the voices of boys doing drills on the Place des Arcades, blinded by the southern light, bothered by the Mediterranean wind, dazed by hopeless, pointless exercises. What had these marching men done with what I'd bestowed on them? They too had been granted love. Where had I gone wrong?

Those were the years I doubted myself. Those were the years when I almost lost hope. What were people doing to one another? It was all so unnecessary.

Aimée, her husband, and their daughter, Renée, fled to Dieulefit to join the Resistance. One thousand five hundred refugees found a safe haven in Dieulefit—Jewish children and adults, artists and writers, Louis Aragon and Elsa Triolet, the German painter Wols. Not one of those refugees was ever betrayed by the inhabitants. Not a single one was deported. Every time their pursuers swept through the village, those in hiding would be spirited away through the night, on carts and wagons and along secret mountain paths and wild boar tracks, to other farms. Farther and farther they traveled, into the mountains and valleys, into the gorges of the Baronnies, into the perilous side valleys of the Eygues, along the twisting Angèle valley, into the depths of the Oules and the hidden folds of the Lance. With the help of council secretary Jeanne Barnier, Aimée faked over a thousand sets of identity papers.

That strong backbone. In such circumstances, it takes an inner light to cope. Courage and resilience, honor and empathy, that stretched far back into her childhood.

The war passed, and Aimée returned to her valley near Nyons at the foot of Mont Vaux. Then one day, after twenty years spent between the four mountains, summer meadows and winter fires, vines and streams, olive trees and lavender fields, apricot groves and purple-flowering Judas trees, my sister Death came along. She took away Aimée's singing milk boy to continue his journey elsewhere. His name was Jean-Marie.

Next, Fate took her daughter and her son-in-law, hurling them off a road into a ravine. Even now, as I look into Aimée's heart, beating in her chest as she moves back and forth across the old patinaed tiles between the stove and the table, her hands reach automatically for four sets of cutlery before she realizes she needs only one.

Hearts, you see, are like beautiful, perfectly glazed earthenware cups at first, but over the years they get cracked and nicked. Hearts break once, twice, repeatedly, and each time you do your best to put them back together again, trying to live with the wounds, patching them up with hope and tears. How I admire you for not giving up on me.

I inspected Aimée's heart and saw it was shattered. That was my doing. I do not spare people. I force them to depend on what they hate and to lose what they need.

The nicks in the cup continued to grow deeper, and occasionally Aimée would cut her lip on a sharp edge. Her skin wept when she heard a song, caught a whiff of sheep's milk and the earthy smell of autumn soil; whenever she unwittingly rolled over onto the cold, empty side of the bed; each time the bells of St. Vincent's struck eleven with the same short, sharp metallic chime as at Jean-Marie's funeral.

Neither love nor death recognizes such a thing as justice. What wouldn't I have done to change my nature? I was ashamed, and maybe it was that shame that made me bend over the cradle to avoid the sight of the sharp edges and Aimée's weeping skin. Maybe what followed was the consequence, the price I had to pay.

"Hello, Marie-Jeanne," I whispered.

2

The Sweet, Unexpected Taste of Despair

As a precaution I kept my hands behind my back so that I wouldn't accidentally touch the little baby and burden it too prematurely with yearning and searching. My time—for we all have our time—comes later in someone's life.

All of us are products of circumstances, characteristics, elements. Whatever you wish to call them. Whichever tiny word you choose to capture our unfathomable nature: Love, Passion, Creativity, Lust, Intelligence, Humor, Fear, to mention but a few of us. You hang us on a particular peg. Not too many syllables, not too long. Sometimes I wonder why we don't have different names.

We all have our chance to make our mark on a human life and to bestow arbitrary amounts of desire or reason, patience or restlessness. Every one of us, even my horrible distant relative Aunt Logic and her ludicrously rational family—Reason, Pragmatism, Conscience, and a handful of equally grim characters—seizes the opportunity to pour as much of ourself into an individual as we see fit.

The bad news is that there are no rules. Each of us is as hasty or earnest or reckless as the moment and our mood dictate, our gift ranging from a smattering of passion dispensed from pinched fingertips to a suffocating wagonload. This often results in the most improbable combinations. You'll know such people: the miserable but amusing comedian, the professor utterly absorbed in his dry profession, the woman who longs for never-ending passion yet remains unwaveringly true, and, of course, all those whose breasts are riven by two, three, four, even eight competing souls.

Another not-so-good piece of news is that we very rarely gather around a child's cradle, seesaw, bed, or playpen to have a sensible discussion. There are simply too many things to do in the world, and do we really look like Sleeping Beauty's seven fairy godmothers?

Quite.

Sometimes Reason and Logic visit a baby only after Desire and Pleasure have already caused a number of problems. These babies will often grow up to be charming characters who throw themselves headlong into disastrous decisions, just for the hell of it; even the best advice won't deter them from taking this path. In other places and at other times, however, Pleasure arrives so late on the scene that the person is entering the penultimate stages of their journey. In a fit of generosity, she introduces an overdue touch of intensity to a flagging existence. This can sometimes lead previously sensible young fossils to take a leap of faith and enjoy things they have always denied themselves. It's as if a window has been smashed open somewhere and they're suddenly desperate to drink in the unfamiliar, wonderfully fresh air. From the outside it might look as if they are deliberately running away from security into the arms of ruin, but that isn't true. Those moody beasts Curiosity and Desire cast the first stone and then watch from a safe distance as a hitherto straightforward life suddenly performs a grandiose, crazy pirouette.

The important thing to remember is that whichever of us is the first to leave their mark most influences an infant's character. They set the tone and lay the foundations.

A short aside about my methods

A few young people in Nyons had been teetering on the edge of adulthood. Their wonderful mental confusion made them most receptive to the many and varied effects of my powers. Everything lit up inside them and they realized they wanted far more from life than to have their own room, hang upside down on the swing, sit around campfires, and never have to go to bed early. In those warm August nights of 1958, as they looked up at the fading meteorites of the Perseid shower, they felt a tugging inside them, and suddenly there was much they could no longer express.

The nights when wishes are made—that's what people call those nights, and you have to choose your wishes carefully because they will come true.

I wandered among the girls and boys as the stars rained down on the feast of St. Lawrence. The night air settled warmly on faces and on bare arms and legs, heavy with the scents of thyme, rosemary, lavender, sage, and mint. They sensed they were entering a sweet, forbidden realm that the adults had been guarding so jealously from them.

Under cover of darkness I touched these souls in passing as they began to take notice of their bodies. A shoulder here, a mouth or a hand there. For the rest of their lives these would be their most love-sensitive spots, which explains why people walk hand in hand, hug, and kiss each other on the lips.

Oh, and in case anyone is tempted to ask: No, I never left my mark on someone's backside. Never. So there's no point in tapping someone on the bottom in the hope that their eyes will sparkle with delight. The same is true of certain other parts of the body that are within the purview of my capricious sister Lust. I'll tell you about her, but only briefly and not now.

Lust and Curiosity like to sail along in my slipstream, sowing a degree of chaos into someone's life when they get trapped between love and desire, seriousness and fun. Between you and me, Lust and Curiosity tend to be deceitful, blasphemous, vain, inexplicably good-humored and at the same time devilishly thin-skinned. They have no respect for anything, least of all for Love or Logic. The only one of us they respect is Death, because they are scared of her. All of us are. Our beautiful, never-aging elder sister is capable of silencing us. She tidies up after our mischief and removes all the burdens we have placed on a single soul in a single life. Only in her presence do Lust and Curiosity stare silently at the ground like the rest of us.

I single out you humans with a mark you cannot see and then bring you together. From that moment on, you will look and long for one another. I give you strength and hope, I make you do things and be there for one another, I create space for stupidity and generosity, patience and imagination.

It is you who make love visible in everything you think and say, everything you do or choose not to. But I am the one who turns you into searchers. One day, one night, you become lovers and you begin to yearn—but for whom, you do not know.

I come and go at will. None of you can pin me down. No one.

Or so I thought.

Suddenly the cicadas fell silent. And *she* came.

"You're too early, my dear," said my sister Death as she stepped closer through the flowering bougainvillea. The bees fashioned caps for themselves from the chalices of wisteria flowers. The wind dropped.

"So are you," I said. I'd been contemplating mending the last intact area of Aimée's broken heart. There was someone up in the hills around Condorcet, and the two of them . . .

Sister Death was already heading for the open kitchen door. I saw Aimée straighten and glance toward us. Slowly she wiped her hands on a tea towel hanging from the belt she wore over her dress. She rested her hands on the table to the left and right of the plain blue plate and looked out at the cradle and the mountains. She stared through Death as my sister strode toward her.

"*I* don't choose the timing. They do that themselves," Death said quietly.

"But the child will be alone. Come back tomorrow or, even better, in a few years."

"She has the olive tree."

"The tree can't warm her milk."

"It will shelter her from the sun and the rain. That will be enough. And if it isn't, I shall return."

"May I say something?" said the olive tree as Death crossed the threshold.

"No," I begged under my breath.

"Jean-Marie?" Aimée whispered as Death stopped in front of her.

The blue plate fell to the floor and then, so did Aimée.

Sister Death caught and held Aimée with the arms of the man who used to sing to her, and her soul breathed its last in them. Released from the body, the soul swelled and unfolded into light, the light increasing and expanding.

"A great soul," Death whispered, gazing up at the light that was more powerful than her, stronger than death. "She loved. Thank you."

I was still standing beside the cradle when the soft, warm light enveloped me—the same light I dispense in infinite forms. My hands, I realized, were no longer knitted behind my back but resting tensely on the cradle's edge.

Marie-Jeanne had grabbed one of my fingers in her tiny fist and was clasping it tightly. The child was staring at me. Her wide blue eyes were studying my face with no trace of fear.

I'd never experienced anything like it. Never before had anyone held on to me, let alone seen me—my essence, my nature, my countenance, my form. It had only ever been the other way around: Love can see inside every person, to the very bottom of their being.

But this was Marie-Jeanne.

"Now you belong to her," said the olive tree, "and she'll cause you no end of trouble."

The smart-ass was really getting on my nerves.

Who else can love

Olive trees can love, of course. I'd almost forgotten that. I've been doing what I do for so long, for such an incredibly long time. A few centuries ago, I'd leaned against this still-young and fragile trunk when the valleys and hills around Nyons contained nothing but isolated *bories* and remote monasteries, when the first houses and the fort, the bridge, the donjon, and St. Vincent's church were taking shape in the town. *Pardon,* but it's impossible to recall every tree.

I always remember people, though, each and every one. I visit everyone at least once on their journey (some two or three times: I don't like to be stingy) and sometimes—I've adopted this habit over the millennia—I will drop by once in a while, purely to take stock. Yes, I'm inquisitive. I like to know what they make of what I give them. They. You. Humans in general.

Most of you have an amazing gift for messing up what is actually so very easy. All you have to say is "Oh hello, Love. Come inside and make yourself at home. Know how long you'll be here? One night? A month? What . . . all my life? Okay then . . . I'll need to get ready for better, for worse, for richer, for poorer. Well, if you have second thoughts and start to leave again . . . fine . . . on your way out I'll call out, 'Thanks for coming. I've loved and so I've truly lived, even if only for one night.' "

It's never that simple, though. People don't notice me, even when I'm right in front of them, pointing madly at the person with whom they could taste what love is. Light, strong, bright, dark, soothing, tormenting, searching, and finding: I am all of everything, the one true meaning that makes life worth seizing with both hands.

And yet I'm invisible. I only become visible through your actions. Love is an occupation, though also . . .

But let's get to the point I've been so deftly avoiding: my accidental touch with Marie-Jeanne and its total unpredictability—for Fate, for the universe, for lovers.

I can assure you, though, that I needed to set the scene so that we could get to know each other. Let's fold up time (even though it hates having this done to it), for why else would we gather together in this book if we hadn't already decided that books are precisely where magic, the great wide world, miracles, and good explanations may all converge? Are books not the last remaining place for otherwise inconceivable encounters between different people, different periods, different landscapes, and different emotions?

If Love is the poetry of the senses, books are the poetry of the impossible.

3

Books Cause Nothing but Trouble

Marie-Jeanne Claudel was almost ten years old when she cut off one of her long plaits with Francis's smallest pair of garden shears. When her foster mother, Elsa—who was the wife of Nyons deliveryman and secondhand trader Francis Meurienne, a state of affairs she'd been bemoaning for decades—asked why in the name of Jesus, Mary, and Joseph she had done such a [*add your own expletive*] thing, Marie-Jeanne was incapable of properly explaining her actions. It was somehow related to Loulou, though. Blond Loulou, the third of Nyons's baker Claudine Raspail's five daughters. Loulou had gotten so upset comparing her own short, blond locks to Marie-Jeanne's long, dark hair that she'd had no option but to hack off her own to make her friend feel better.

"And did that make the envious little goose feel any better?"

"I think so. She burst out laughing, at least, and she still laughs every time she sees me. And she's not a goose. I think she's as pretty and snuggly as a brioche."

Elsa barked several more unquotable swear words in her finest Provençal dialect to hide her satisfaction and pride at

Marie-Jeanne's awfully kind but extremely stupid gesture to protect her new friend. We shall discover later why Elsa has two faces but chooses to show the world the uglier of the two.

She considered it fundamentally detrimental to the formation of a little girl's character to be strikingly pretty before her seventeenth birthday. She matter-of-factly snipped off the second plait, washed Marie-Jeanne's remaining hair with homemade lavender-scented goat milk soap (gently, albeit with much grumbling and cursing), and evened out any protruding strands and meddlesome flyaway hairs with scissors she normally used for trimming the threads of lace veils and Spanish fans. (Elsa was proud that her farsightedness did not prevent her from producing exquisite items for bridal dowries.)

Weddings were another thing Elsa officially regarded as a poetic delusion, even as she sat in Francis's barn at night, secretly sobbing into botched lace tissues because she wanted only the very best for the couples, the very best a lifetime could offer. She also hoped they had more trust in love than she did, because . . . She preferred not to think this thought through to the end. She was pretty good at interrupting her thoughts just as they got interesting—for example, when they turned to her own lot.

"So," said Elsa, placing the scissors back in her lace-making case. "You look like Jean Seberg now. She too had hair like little matches."

"Like *who*?"

Elsa rummaged intently in her lace-making kit for a second, but now it was out, so she had no choice but to plow on.

"Oh, a poor girl, an American actress. She played the leading role in *Bonjour Tristesse* before falling in love with a writer. Everyone knows male authors are all liars and drunkards, and that's when her misery began."

She hoped Marie-Jeanne would take the hint that their conversation about hair and tragic love affairs was now over, but the girl wouldn't let things lie.

"*Bonjour Trist*—?"

Elsa sighed. How did other—that is, birth—mothers handle these situations? By beating around the bush until their daughters eventually found out for themselves and accused them of never having told them the whole truth?

"It's a book, actually. By Françoise Sagan." She was determined to avoid going into any further detail about the previous decade's most scandalous novel. She needed to change the subject. But to what? Oh yes, to a piece of information she'd picked up from tradesmen at the Bar du Centre, run by Luc le Marseillais. "Sagan loved driving fast cars barefoot. She was very young when she wrote her first book. Only a few years older than you."

"Can I be a writer too?"

Somehow, thought Elsa, this conversation had taken a wrong turn. "Better not."

"Why?"

Damn! Where was Francis when you actually needed him?

"How do you like your new hairstyle?"

"Why's it better not to be a writer?"

Hmm, thought Elsa. She could tell her foster daughter what other mothers probably hammered home to their daughters: "A writer? Seriously? How would you ever find a husband?" Or: "There are already more than enough books in the world. Why add to the pile?" Or what they'd been told at school in her day, though she'd never believed it herself: "Too much reading makes you dowdy." This was thought to be particularly true of young women. And as to where writing might ultimately lead . . . that didn't bear thinking about. If Marie-Jeanne became an author, the only time she'd enter the kitchen would be to light a cigarette on the gas stove.

"You see, when all's said and done, books cause nothing but trouble."

"You shouldn't say things like that," said Francis, who had just hobbled into the kitchen from outside, his jolly paunch preceding the rest of him. A grin split his tanned face under thick, dark eyebrows. "Books have nothing to do with it."

"Why not? It's never too early for a girl to learn that she needs to stay away from certain things and people. It would've been good if someone had told *me* that."

Touché! Elsa couldn't help herself. She could tell she'd hurt Francis because the corners of his mouth twitched. His mouth was usually shaped like a paper boat, the ends of his lips always arcing upward in genial joie de vivre. Unless she said something nasty to him, in which case the little boat would capsize on his beloved face.

Elsa grumbled. Francis sighed.

And Marie-Jeanne? She ran a finger silently over the scissors. The blades were curved like a stork's beak, and its plumage and the finger holes were delicately gilded.

Marie-Jeanne imagined that writers could do whatever they wanted. Drive cars barefoot, become a drunkard (whatever that might be, it sounded tempting), and make up any story they liked about the world—with a happy ending every time. In any case, that's what she would do. How wonderful it would be to rescue people in books! Also, it would always be summertime. Summer was always a long time coming, apart from in books.

Outside the cicadas were silent, their song yet to commence. This was one of the Drôme Provençale's ancient, unexplained mysteries: Did cicadas usher in the summer with their chorus, or did summer make the cicadas sing?

A potentially indispensable note on Elsa Malbec

Elsa Malbec. It isn't easy to come into the world under such an explicit name—"Malbec" literally means "nasty beak." Elsa had cultivated this legacy by saying nasty things from a young age. Initially she'd listened to her parents and, later, to how people who had lived through one or two wars talked in the streets—aggressively, loudly, in one of the local Occitan dialects, using expressions from the battles and the Bible and their strict upbringing, always with a clenched fist, even at mealtimes, when fists would lie at the ready alongside stoneware plates.

It had nothing to do with her childless marriage to Francis Meurienne, the deliveryman and collector of weird objects. Incidentally, Elsa loved him desperately and was grateful that this short, hobbling man tolerated and accepted her—an unattractive but at least useful crooked thing, she of the nasty beak who couldn't help biting, taunting, spurning, and setting herself with all her might against tenderness, intimacy, and love.

Love—no way!

Love, oh, love!

. . .

Elsa needed me so badly and yet she hated this neediness. She didn't want to fall for that stupid tyrant Love. To her I was an idiotic, villainous cow who laughed at people, all the more so someone like her, as stout as a crippled olive tree.

How was she to know that I have precious little interest in a person's outward appearance or character? I see what is essential: the capacity of someone's heart for love. As a rule, heart, mouth, and mind are linked in only the most roundabout way—a person's love may express itself harshly, with an impressive array of swear words, or in silent, shy despair.

I sometimes wished someone would invent a *dictionnaire d'amour*—a lover's dictionary listing all the weird and wonderful ways in which humans show their love. An inordinate number of men choose to repair things; other people frantically rebuff compliments, and still others stubbornly conceal their love so as not to pester anyone. A dictionary—yes! Of course, it could never be comprehensive.

Back to Elsa, though. She was about five foot three, possessed a body as soft as a pillow and strong arms, a magnificent old Italian face (have a look at old masters like Lorenzo Lotto, or imagine Mona Lisa in her midforties with a more deeply furrowed brow), and had distant relatives in Italy who would occasionally send her a leg of ham by mail. She wanted to be both independent and less anxious. She found Francis's deep love for her terrifying because after twenty years she was starting to need it. And if she needed it, then aargh! she'd be even more anxious not to lose it. Not to lose Francis and his paunch and his lame foot, his wrists and the sharp tan lines drawn by the rolled-up sleeves of a sweater smelling of sunshine. There was no way she wanted that. She didn't want to live with that anxiety and then go crazy and tie herself in knots trying not to lose that love. That was no way to live.

It wasn't even as if my beastly cousin Fear had bestowed much of her gift on Elsa. It was Imagination who gave her panic attacks, while pure Logic observed this unholy alliance in desperation, too timid to intervene.

Once, I touched Elsa's hands. The skill of lace-making had already entered her life, endowing her with sensitivity, precision, and unstinting patience, and I had held those skillful hands, gently prying open her baby fists and placing in them everything she would ever need. Young Elsa Malbec had clenched her fists again, and the only other time she had relented was the night the still-young Francis took her hand demurely and she felt the softness of his whole being.

Before Marie-Jeanne fell into her life, Elsa had reckoned—every day—with the possibility that Francis might not come home to this house built of fieldstone and hewn rock at the southern end of the Eygues valley, surrounded by orchards and olive trees and steeped in the fragrance of the Nyons soap factory when the wind came from that direction.

Why should he come home to her? That is why she was so nasty to him. And because love never lasts forever, whatever you might or might not do, so . . . By this point, Elsa Malbec would be so tangled up in her thoughts that she would turn to something else, furiously making lace or marching to her well-tended vegetable patch to drown slugs in a jug of beer.

Sometimes Elsa would bury her face in one of Francis's blue work sweaters and inhale its aroma, the smell of the man himself and the countryside so irreversibly wedded to his skin. She would feel such a fierce pang in her chest that she could barely hold back her tears. She was concerned that Francis would spy the salty stains and realize that she was already grieving for him, her husband and her refuge, when he was still alive. He was her entire world, and that was why she hated love and him and most of all herself. Elsa couldn't abide being in love.

Francis. Pronouncing his name, one's lips automatically formed a kiss, and she said it over and over again when she was alone in the barn.

And the child—this child, still brimming with the same amazement and enthusiasm for life with which she had entered their house. She celebrated and embraced everything attentively, with devotion. Yes, that beautiful old-fashioned word "devotion," which described something Elsa knew only from books. (Or from the nine or ten books she'd read so far of her own accord, including the one by the wild and free Sagan that had taught her more about love than she desired to know.)

To Elsa, Marie-Jeanne showed a devotion and a fearless love for the stars and the clouds and the various types of rain. She was devoted to flowers and seeds and the different-shaped droppings left by rodents (what a pain!) and wild boar. Devoted to the sucking sounds on the riverside on a rainy day when someone inadvertently slipped into the Eygues, to the noises of winter (the wind whistling around the corner of the house, the blue crickle-crackle of flames in the hearth!). Devoted to watching Elsa's fingers as she made lace in the winter months, when time slowed and gave a gray-blue glaze to the afternoons. How well too this child understood what Elsa was doing, the way her fingers could work tenderness and hope into something as ordinary as lace.

One day, the way the girl called her "Mommy" melted Elsa's heart into bright, shimmering, golden mead. How it hurt and how good it felt and how painful it was.

What option did Elsa have but to be stern with her? Stern, so it would hurt less if the girl were ever to leave.

The child's love for her foster mother caused Elsa to feel her meager life was slipping away, running through her fingers like a slender thread she couldn't grasp. At its end was a predator, lurking outside beyond the thicket of the coming years.

What if she died without telling Francis she loved him?

She sometimes thought that she would dig herself out of her grave to tell him so for the very first time.

4

How a Man Found a Child One Day

"Marie can lend me a hand today," Francis eventually said.

"If you like. The stupid lump is only getting in my way," Elsa mumbled.

Why say that? Elsa's reason butted in. *You don't mean it.*

Because I want to make it easy for the two of them to go outside together and have adventures. Because I'm a gloomy cloud blocking out the sunshine. Can we drop the subject now, please? Why are you whispering inside my head? Who are you anyway?

(We know: retiring Reason.)

As a bric-a-brac dealer and deliveryman—the word "courier" hadn't yet been invented in late 1960s France—Francis was continually ferrying things from one place to another. He would drive out to the remotest farms in the valleys and on the slopes between Mirabel, Montjoux, Chaudebonne, and Sahune and memorize people's orders (Francis couldn't write fast enough and he read barely any quicker). Then, depending on the state of the roads, he would harness Josephine, his donkey, to the front of the car or argue with his blue 2CV van, Louis the Third, until the engine started up again and it could haul itself along the narrow, rutted tracks.

Francis would squeeze his spherical, pullover-encased paunch behind the steering wheel and carry out the deliveries. Tow bars, distillation flasks, handles for well buckets, and other things for which no one living between the four mountains of Essaillon, Garde Grosse, Saint Jaume, and Vaux would ever willingly set out through the tangled garrigue to Nyons and back. When Francis delivered these items, he would rummage in a sleepy pile in the darkest corner of a barn or farm and stumble across an object longing to return to the outside world. A toothless nutcracker. A blind rocking horse. A triangle without its wand. Dressers. Empty picture frames. Ladles. Battered objects that had lost their usefulness and function but hadn't lost their soul. Something about them touched Francis. Many a time the blue van would crawl back along the bumpy track, the engine shrieking in first gear as the vehicle wound its way up steep hairpin bends into the mountains and then—damn!—spluttered its way down the other side to rescue a forgotten object from the shadows. Wind chimes suffering for lack of a breeze. A coffee roaster only a long-deceased grandfather knew how to operate. Flails and gramophone horns.

Francis Meurienne's farm and its scattered barns on the road from Nyons to Mirabel contained a ragtag collection that will raise plenty of eyebrows when future archaeologists and historians strive to work out what the hell life used to be like in this area.

As a little boy, the youngest of six children, who mercifully escaped his parents' attention, Francis had conceived a gentle and secretive affection for abandoned objects. He took in the things others rejected. Some he repaired, whereas others formed the core of collections designed to allow these rejects to chat among themselves. Objects couldn't communicate of course, but . . . but it was nevertheless a comforting thought.

It had probably slipped his mind that he'd adopted this habit after becoming less useful himself at the age of eight, following an unfortunate encounter between his foot and a winegrower's tractor tire. Had he noted the coincidence, he probably wouldn't have cared very much about it. Francis didn't like overcomplicating things.

He'd never told anyone about these objects, though. Only Marie-Jeanne, only once, and even then, not directly. It wasn't necessary: She understood him instinctively.

Everything was much easier with her. Every time he saw the girl, a fountain of laughter sprang from his chest. *Blub-blub* went this inner spring, bathing his heart in champagne.

He picked up the curled hazelnut plait from the kitchen's tiled floor, wrapped it around his fist, and put it in his pocket. He had decided many years ago to give Marie-Jeanne a small box for when she set out into the wide world beyond the four hills. It would contain all the things she'd treasured as a child.

Back then, Francis had imagined pressed flowers, snail shells, and buzzard feathers, but the box he was filling in the barn had long since swollen into a wooden chest. Marie-Jeanne cherished almost everything. She loved the entire world, even if in his opinion that was neither possible nor sensible.

She loved getting up in the morning and looking out to see whether the summit of Mont Ventoux was visible or veiled in pensive clouds. She loved to lie under her cool bedclothes in the evenings with the window open and listen to the melodies of twilight—the cries of owls and the fading whisper of the forest, so similar to the crashing of ocean waves. She loved the smell of the classroom and the color pebbles turned when she dipped them in well water. She loved Elsa's tomato sauce with black Autrand olives, and the squeak of Francis's old leather shoes on the uneven wooden attic floor of the *mazet*. She loved it when Nyons soap melded itself to the curve of her palm. She loved the echoes of the seven-hundred-year-old bells in Nyons's "apple tower" on a quiet autumn morning when mist and rain clouds drifted over the mountaintops, carrying the noises and sounds of the world far and wide.

She danced with brimstone butterflies as they fluttered about her. After Francis taught her how to play music on a dew-damp blade of grass, she gathered stems of varying length and pitch. She loved it when he changed gears in the tunnel near Nyons and, for a few delicious seconds, Louis the Third's engine roared like a racing car's at the Monaco Grand Prix. She had an infinite and contagious gift for living life to the full.

Marie-Jeanne collected herbs, her favorite letters of the alphabet, pine kernels, and scratched pétanque balls. To his horror she also collected the regional swear words with their colorful Italian tinge that Elsa often blurted out. She took in homeless animals (Francis had been lumbered with three ownerless kittens at once and named them Meeny, Miny, and Moe. As if they didn't have enough pets already with the cheeky little floppy-eared, brown-and-white dog, Tictac, now they had cats too!) and saw faces in trees. Every day sparked some new passion. There was nothing she didn't find beautiful, nothing that wasn't lovable and special to her.

Francis gazed at her with the amazement of a man who had come to fatherhood late in life. He smiled. He couldn't help himself. Marie-Jeanne and a few wandering goats were probably the only creatures who saw him smile so often, his mouth a laughing boat whose bow and stern rode a wave of paternal love.

This was how it had been ever since he had found her lying in her wicker basket on Aimée Claudel's terrace ten years ago in 1958. She was clearly having fun, despite the fact that her grandmother had breathed her last. She was waving her clenched fists in the air "like a miniature Joan of Arc, I'm telling you, Elsa, as if she were trying to say, 'Long live the king! Onward, comrades!' and as if she were holding something, something bright. And you know what was so strange? The cicadas weren't making a sound. Not a single chirp. In midsummer! As if time had stood still." His heart had gone out to her as he stroked the tiny outstretched fist and Marie-Jeanne clung to Francis's rough, mud-encrusted thumb with her free left hand.

Something had happened in that instant.

Something had been . . . *set in motion.*

Francis found he could breathe more freely. He felt warmth and lightness flowing through him. He wanted to make plans. He wanted to go to Elsa and tell her everything on his mind. He wanted to do something one day, come up with an idea that would turn the world upside down. For the very first time he thought he was somehow significant, that he existed.

Then the tiny thing looked at him as if she understood him completely. Everything—yes, even the aspects of himself Francis didn't understand: why he loved Elsa (although there was probably no meaner woman between the Drôme and the Camargue) and why he didn't like talking with people but would chat to flowers and trees and the garrigue with its unruly gorse bushes. Maybe it was because they were like Elsa. They were part of the land, and he was part of her.

When the mayor of Nyons decided that the Resistance fighter Aimée Claudel's orphaned granddaughter ought to stay at Francis and Elsa's with the council paying them a small allowance rather than be sent to a state-run children's home in Lyons, Francis felt relief. Relief that he was allowed to keep the girl who understood him so well.

As Marie-Jeanne grew older and learned to speak, Francis was profoundly moved by her talkativeness and attention to objects and creatures. But he knew that very few others would be understanding of these qualities. After all, he spoke to his car, and most people enjoy lecturing their dogs. Oddly enough, hardly anyone in his entourage found such behavior unusual. But someone who talked to trees?

No sooner was Marie-Jeanne able to toddle around on her chubby little legs than she began to hold regular conversations with the gnarled old olive tree outside her grandmother's house. The *mazet* would be hers one day, but in the meantime Francis took care of matters. Before he went off to make his deliveries, he would put her down on the terrace with a jug of water from the well and a bowl of ratatouille. She would sit there for hours under the tree, leaning back with her hands stretched out behind her and waggling her toes, apparently deep in conversation with her old companion.

. . .

Amazingly, Marie-Jeanne never talked with the olive tree about *that* August day in 1958.

I admit that a long time passed before I pried my finger loose from the clasp of her fist. I was, to put it mildly, in complete shock.

"Now you belong to her," the ancient olive tree predicted. "This will cause no end of trouble."

"What's that supposed to mean?"

"I've no idea, but that's the way it is. You belong to her, but she doesn't belong to you. That's all I can tell you in response to your vague query. But you know it already."

Great. This olive tree was one of the very few survivors on this earth who had all the answers—but only if you asked the right questions. Which is hard, because if you don't know what you're meant to know, you can't ask. You see the conundrum.

So I stuck close to Marie-Jeanne, first, because I wanted to, and second, because I couldn't do otherwise, as she was still clinging to me. The girl didn't even seem to notice, though! After all, she was a tiny human baby and at that stage of our acquaintance, the organ that would later develop into a clever and cultivated brain was still in a state of disorder and transition. Marie-Jeanne dozed off blissfully, and when she woke up, she was greeted by the tree, Francis, and a sublime sense of being alive.

Later, she wanted to find out a thousand other things from the colossal olive tree: What was my mommy like as a girl? What was here before Granny's house? What is tripe? Do birds have favorite branches? Don't beetles get itchy feet?

But it is time to move on.

5

The Art of Diplomacy According to Francis the Bric-a-brac Dealer

"Ooh, they left you such a tiny, battered milk jug and you're still happy!" Elsa had once said after watching Marie-Jeanne hug the olive tree outside her grandmother's house, whisper to it, and scratch the back of its trunk.

Anyone who knew Elsa well could tell from this doubly snide remark that her heart was overflowing with love, however hard she sought to resist the tide of emotion. But Francis didn't know her well; he simply accepted her the way she was. A different Elsa would not have been his. Francis was happy. With which other companion could he walk in the hills without too much conversation, enjoying the scent of wild thyme with a tinge of lemon, light, and sun?

"Have you finished now?" he asked, the plait still in his pocket.

"You're never finished with this girl," Elsa muttered. "Anyway, off you both go."

"I brought home a Munster cheese and some fresh bread for tonight. We could put it in the oven with some cumin and—" he began.

"That sounds revolting!" she said.

"It isn't. You wouldn't recognize something good if it walked up and punched you on the nose."

"That's true. I'd scarcely have married you if I did."

Francis picked up his cap and set it on top of Marie-Jeanne's short-cropped hair. *As soft as the down on a chick,* he thought, *and just as vulnerable.* He hoped his wife would stop being so nasty someday. Not to him—he was used to that; sometimes he felt like a pincushion. No, she should be less prickly toward the girl, even if the child didn't seem to register Elsa's aggression. That was odd too.

"We're going to drive to Grignan today," he tried again. "We're going to pick up something and take it to—"

"Yeah yeah," Elsa said. "Tell your checkered handkerchief."

"Thank you for my beautiful haircut, Maman," Marie-Jeanne said. Her kiss brushed Elsa's cheek so quickly that her foster mother couldn't dodge it, as she usually did with such displays of affection. Then the girl dashed after Francis, who had a good word with Louis the Third, patted its blue wings, and started the engine.

"My name is Elsa," she cried at Marie-Jeanne's retreating back, "and I'm not your mommy!"

The girl didn't look back as she and Tictac got into the van. It would have surprised Elsa to know that Marie-Jeanne was smiling mischievously with a secret so outrageous that it was better to hide it behind a barely stifled giggle.

Maybe it had something to do with the little sparkle Marie-Jeanne had recently spotted on Elsa's fingers.

Elsa rubbed her cheek, which was still smarting from the kiss. No, she wasn't Marie-Jeanne's mother, much as she would have loved to have been. Why was she the way she was and not a different woman? Who on earth had put her together so wonkily?

I could have explained, but she wouldn't have listened to me, and she'd probably have been more than a little irritated if I'd told her that it was due to the different doses of elements such as Skepticism and Logic, Love and Fear, Pragmatism and Whimsy, struggling to reach an equilibrium inside her. Elsa Malbec would have simply picked up her broom and swept me out of the house.

There was a comfortable silence in the blue van, whose sun-warmed interior exuded aromas of leather, metal, oil, hay, and bundled herbs. The fragrances of life in the midst of nature.

Both Francis and Marie-Jeanne loved the slightly longer route to Grignan along the D538 via Rousset-les-Vignes, Montbrison, and Taulignan, a village where cats prowled the street that curled around the church and explored the vineyards and lush, flowering meadows, the olive groves, the lavender fields, and the tree nurseries. Beyond Nyons, whose center was hemmed in between two slopes, and Venterol, it seemed as if the world suddenly opened up.

Everything was wider and higher here. Marie-Jeanne could see the whole sky, and she glimpsed the mountains of her childhood in the rearview mirror. Everything seemed possible. All she needed to do to find her true vocation was to keep traveling. Soon, around a bend, Grignan castle would rear up unexpectedly out of the landscape.

News of a distant and quicker world came burbling out of the radio—a world that had no impact on them here in this forgotten corner of France. One day, the year 1968 would be famous, with a symbolism far surpassing its four succinct figures.

Francis started to sing what he called "The Cicada Song" to summon the summer. He sang in the local dialect, a mixture of Italian and Occitan:

Lou souèu mi fai canta . . .
Your light makes me sing,
Blinded by the heart of your beauty.
Lady Death and mortality.
You are what I wish to be,
Summer never ends.
Lou souèu mi fai canta . . .

Marie-Jeanne joined in. The wonderful objects in the back of the car clattered in time to the bumps in the road, and Tictac dangled his cheeky little droopy ears out the window in the wind. There was a glint of laughter on his face. He was a pleasing hybrid of pinscher, Jack Russell, and some other jaunty ancestor with too much arrogance and too little humility.

They drove through plains and valleys where distances were measured not in miles but in the number of hours it took to cross this luscious land on these winding roads.

"Petitpa?" Marie-Jeanne asked after a while.

Little Papa. Francis loved this strange, cobbled-together name she had given him as soon as she learned to speak. "Hmm?"

"How did Louis the Third get his name?"

"He's my third 2CV van. I got my first when I was twenty-two."

"How old are you now?"

"As old as an olive tree."

"I can believe that! Know why?"

"No."

"Because a tree never reveals its age either."

"Oh, right."

"And why do you call Josephine Josephine when Maman's around, but Fino when she isn't?"

"Did you eat a why machine for breakfast?"

"Yeah, it was disguised as a slice of brioche with apricot jam on it. A real tastebud tickler." She paused before continuing, "Um, I think you turned twenty-two yesterday."

Francis sighed. That was another thing with Marie-Jeanne: She wasn't very good at lying. No good at all, in fact. If she didn't learn, it was going to land her in a lot of trouble. But how was he supposed to teach her to lie convincingly when everyone frowned on lying and yet constantly did it? How did other parents deal with this? After all, some lies were useful, hurt no one, and let in a little sunlight.

"Listen, Marie, you shouldn't lie."

"Never? Not even to dress up the truth a little?"

"No, never."

"So why *do* you call Josephine Josephine when Maman's around and Fino when she isn't? Isn't that dressing up the truth?"

Francis considered this. "When we bought Fino, Maman thought he was a girl, but because she can't bear not being right, Fino the donkey is Josephine to her. That isn't a lie. It's . . . diplomacy. Diplomats know that everyone has their own version of the truth and respect it."

"Oh," the girl said, scratching Tictac as she pondered this.

Phew, Francis thought. *By the skin of my teeth.*

Marie-Jeanne was staring out at the fields of yellow sunflowers, the silvery-green olive groves, and the vineyards that in a few months' time would produce plum-colored Côtes du Rhône. There was a purplish flash of blooming lavender fields in the distance, beyond the town of Grignan, which would rise up out of the plain like a crown any minute now.

"You beauties for the eye," she whispered. She stuck her hand out the open window and wiggled her fingers in the gentle breeze.

"Finger bliss," she said, kissing her hand and waving it outside again.

She does that a lot, thought Francis. *She sticks her hand out and seems to caress the summery air.* Exactly as she'd been clutching the air the day he found her. When time stood still and something happened in the expanding space.

"So you love her," Marie-Jeanne observed.

"Who, Josephine? Of course."

Of course, my foot! Of course Francis knew she meant Elsa rather than the donkey, but what did a child know about love?

Marie-Jeanne understood what she knew about love with her senses rather than her intellect. She knew for example that love feels like the sensation you get when the aroma from the bakery tickles your nose at half past five in the morning, when the windows are steamed up from the heat from the embers in the oven, and when the bakery lamps shine out into the blue-black morning. An open bakery in the morning is one of hope's most beautiful guises.

"Don't you want to know what we're going to pick up in Grignan?" Francis hastened to ask.

"Summer?"

What a lovely idea! thought Francis. He would pick up

summer and spread it throughout the mountains, especially in Saint-Ferréol-Trente-Pas and Valouse, where carpets of lavender rolled down the hillsides like ski jumps. *"Hello, Madame Bonifat. I've brought the summer for your lavender. I know it's come a bit late this year, but we've had trouble with deliveries. It's not been easy since summer unionized."*

"Bibles," Francis announced proudly. "Direct from the printing works below the castle. For our priest at St. Vincent's, and as a gift for the bridal couples."

Marie-Jeanne's eyes peered out skeptically from under the peak of Francis's cap. Her suspicion stemmed from growing up in a household where neither Elsa nor Francis set much store by religious education.

"Bibles? That isn't a very good present. Everyone knows the words by heart," she finally ventured. "Why doesn't Father give them a book they haven't read? How about *Bonjour Tristesse* by that author who drove fast cars in her bare feet?"

Francis struggled to keep a straight face. "Most people don't have enough money for books. Also, you read them once and then what? Books are like . . . villas in Saint Tropez."

"Big, beautiful, and awfully lonely and unpopular in winter?" Marie-Jeanne asked. Tictac was perching on her lap now, panting as he concentrated on the view through the windshield.

"Something like that. They stand around and are nice to look at, but those arrogant Parisians use them only once a year, and . . . not everyone can afford one. I don't really know much about books, though."

Francis had nothing against books, he really didn't—only against the words they contained. They could be so monstrous. That's right: They were monsters he couldn't understand, and yet all the same they nagged at him because they made him feel he was missing out on something.

He felt stupid every time he studied Monsieur Mussigmann's displays in that newfangled Fernand Nathan bookstore chain on the Place des Arcades. He didn't know anything about the people who wrote these things and, well, you didn't want every Tanguy, Didier, and Armand telling you about the life you were passing up out there. And yet these harmless-looking, rectangular paper things did seem to contain something important. Francis felt excluded, and to his astonishment this thought caused him a lot of pain.

Nyons did in fact have its very own writer. René Barjavel, the baker's son. From what Francis had heard, many of his novels were set in a weird, completely electric future where people did terrible things to nature and movies were delivered directly to your home. There was also a worldwide machine that supplied everyone with everything they needed—ready-made opinions so they didn't have to think so much, and synthetic food. A dream machine. However, one day it stopped working, and a new society grew up in the Baronnies area near Nyons, laboriously reacquiring the knowledge that had enabled them to live autonomously up until the machine's invention.

These writers come up with some very strange ideas, thought Francis.

6

Fate Is a Nasty Piece of Work

Francis looked out at the countryside through Louis the Third's clip-up side windows. It was an absurd idea that change might ever disconnect people from the plains and mountains, the rocks and the vines, from the labor of their hands and the silence of these timeless valleys. How had the baker's son come up with these things? What did he know that others couldn't imagine even after pickling their brains in pastis? What Francis knew for certain was that the man put him in a bad mood.

Meanwhile, Marie-Jeanne was thinking hard. Her foster father could usually tell from the way she would poke a fine strand of hair into her ear. Now, though, she could only tug at her short locks.

"Hold on a second," Francis said, wedging his knees under the steering wheel and handing her a soft paintbrush he'd dug out from behind his seat. He rested his elbow on the windowsill again. (Like all 2CV drivers, he had bruises on his left arm from wedging the misbehaving window open.)

The girl was already raptly tickling the inside of her left ear with the brush.

"Well," she said after a while, "if they're too expensive and no one reads them twice, then the priest would do better to buy a hundred different books so all the married couples could pass them around. Then you could collect all the books and use Louis the Third to take them to the next in line."

Something inside Francis went *ding*. It was very quick and he almost missed it, so to make sure this obtuse deliveryman got the message, it did it twice more. *Ding! Ding!*

Francis cleared his throat. He'd take care of those *ding*s later.

"I'll tell you something you don't know," he said. He'd read very little, but stories still found a way to get through to him. That was the magic of word of mouth: It found first one ear, then another, and just carried on traveling.

And so, as they rattled past the vineyards in Louis the Third—nicknamed "the Hovercraft" because it could transport six hundred eggs along the narrow, bumpy tracks without breaking a single one—Francis Meurienne told the story of Philippa of Montmorin. Raised in a noble household, the young lady decided one day to liberate the county of Nyons from the Duchy of Savoy. Sword in hand, she rode out on horseback and gathered an army of farmers around her. She managed to free Gap, the Baronnies, and the local dioceses from their northern occupiers. Philippa became known as Philis, and the people of liberated Dauphiné regarded her as their equivalent of Joan of Arc. She was a friend of the Marquise de Sévigné, one of the greatest letter writers of her time, who lived with her daughter in Grignan. The marquise's fifteen hundred letters gave more details about life three hundred years ago than the prim and proper accounts of gentleman authors. Grignan castle also contained a library.

Marie-Jeanne closed her eyes and smiled as Francis told his story. Not that he knew, but she had heard the dinging noise.

They fell silent and continued their journey through a landscape where a new fragrance invaded the car every few yards. Rosemary, spring water, dry grass, a wood fire, the scent of blossoms. It was as if the land were getting ready, reaching out to welcome the summer that would soon arrive—at long last!

Francis was lost in all the thoughts triggered by that *ding*. Books, life, that high-pitched sound. Thoughts written down by people you didn't know that gave you an inkling of what all the people you *did* know were keeping from you. *Hmm*. These thoughts might have been ludicrous, but suddenly a plan was taking shape in his mind. Unless that plum brandy old Gégé from Les Pilles had served him had been past its best . . .

"Petitpa," Marie-Jeanne said earnestly, interrupting his helpless, rattling thoughts and turning to him with those eyes that could see deep inside him, "you've come up with an idea, and it's a good one."

Not for the first time, Francis wondered how she managed to scatter his fears. He felt completely transparent in the beam of her gaze. What she found when she looked inside him didn't seem quite as bad as he always thought it was. Not half as bad. How odd. How wonderful.

And as if Fate were waving and shouting, "Hello, over here!" to him, Grignan rose up out of the plain, shining like a gold button in the rocky land, as Francis Meurienne the collector finished hatching his madcap plan.

A brief and not very positive glimpse of Fate's everyday activities

Fate is a little man with an outsized head, hunched over the map of world affairs, muttering to himself, manipulating time, events, and human beings this way and that with lightning hands, thinking that his actions might somehow impress Chance, Wonder, and Hope. To me, Love, he has given no special powers, which is perhaps the most important thing—if not the only thing—you need to know about this boorish character. I can only act within the range of my possibilities, which means endowing people with the capacity to love as well as a lover's patience and desire. What people do with those gifts is their business. They can demonize me, trivialize desire, and satirize despair, but just like -isms, none of these -izes gets us very far.

Anyway . . . I can wound and I can heal, and yes, there were even times when I was proclaimed a remedy—just think of the fountain of youth. But those times are long gone. All gone, damn it! Still, with a single kiss I can resolve decades of suffering and waiting (another thing that drives Time crazy).

I can make a soul buried alive in the wrong marriage suddenly rise again in the right embrace, shedding their premature living death as if this gradual withering away beside the wrong person had never happened. (Thanks a lot, Lady Death says sarcastically.)

I can make people shortsighted, circumspect, or clairvoyant; I would have made a wonderful optician for the soul. I can provide the final push that allows someone to cover the last few yards to their intended one. The only thing I can't do is enable couples to identify each other early enough, just as intelligence cannot bring someone to their senses nor boredom kill a person, hard though it may try.

Fate, however, is capable of putting people through hell and sticking plenty of hurdles in the paths of lovers. They sit there, thinking: *Life is one long litany of disasters, trials, and tests of our courage and perseverance.* Then if by chance they are actually happy, they will only realize this in hindsight. People should count themselves lucky if nothing much happens in their lives. . . .

Another thing the little man can do is sprinkle omens. And boy, does he do it! The gust of wind that flicks a curtain in a mythically significant way at just the right moment, leading someone to interpret an idea that just occurred to them—*I'm going to move out of this house; I'm going to open a carpet shop*—as a positive signal. Music too. The song that opens up our heart at precisely the wrong time, but it's the right song, sending someone off in a particular direction and into the arms of the next stroke of Fate.

And by golly did he love sprinkling omens—the beast!—and pretending that things were full of significance.

7

A Woman's Glow

Francis mulled the idea over and over in his mind. He went to bed with it, got up with it, and took it with him on his delivery trips. In early May 1968 he stood on the Place des Arcades and watched people bustling back and forth between old Blanc the butcher's, the café, the pharmacy, and the bookshop.

From experience he knew that time opened doors one moment only to slam them shut the next. There hadn't been any fruit shops when he was young because everyone had their own orchard. Then, one day, fruit shops had appeared, and so had market stalls outside the fort and the Château Montauban, displaying beef tomatoes, artichokes, dried verbena leaves, and cherries, apricots, and apples from the valley bottom. At the same time, there were fewer and fewer saddleries. No one rode or put a horse before their cart anymore because everyone drove around in cars. So people opened garages and learned their way around the belly of a car, but they no longer knew how to harness a donkey without its biting their nose off.

Francis Meurienne had a long, hard think about these doors of time.

Meanwhile Loulou Raspail, the third daughter of the baker who ran Au Fournil in rue Philis de la Charce—no, not the one belonging to the Achard-Barjavel family, into which the writer with a liking for dystopian science fiction had been born; that bakery was farther up toward the fort, and Au Fournil was the one behind the butcher's and delicatessen shop, whose olive tapenade was so delicious that you felt like getting down on your knees and offering heartfelt thanks to the gods for creating Tanche olives—had realized that no one had ever done anything so absurdly sublime for her as Marie-Jeanne had.

Loulou therefore decided with impeccable logic that Marie-Jeanne must be her best friend. Since the business with the "off-cut plait," as Loulou called it, the two of them had spent every chore-free moment in each other's company. They made a fine couple—one, Marie-Jeanne, coursing with the warmth and energy that allowed her to embrace life so warmly, and the other, Loulou, whose emotional highs and lows went hand in hand with an unshakable optimism. For Loulou every tomorrow held enormous promise. Today was awful? *Tant pis,* tomorrow would be fine. Together they had an amazing effect on people. The hate-filled became gentle, the arrogant human, and melancholics smiled.

How happy people are before they fall in love for the first time.

Anyway, Marie-Jeanne was having breakfast with the baker, his wife, and their five daughters at a respectable hour on their morning off. It was a Thursday, which was also the day when schools were closed. The baker's wife, for once not wearing her blue-and-white striped apron over her suit and freshly curled hair, placed a little crocheted cozy on every soft-boiled egg, and the two friends listened to the older girls' conversations. Their voices sounded like the twittering of morning birds to Marie-Jeanne. Little bustards and robins.

Sometimes she longed for sisters of her own, but she wasn't aggrieved by her fate. The reverse was true: She had lost two boring plaits, but in return she had gained five sisters smelling of fresh baguette and crispy croissants.

(Thanks, says Fate at the end of this moment.)

Noëlle, Martine, and Madeleine were chirruping away about school and an "impossible" boy called Benoît from Les Pilles. Someone else by the name of Jimi Hendrix kept cropping up as they chatted, giggled, and dropped hints. Loulou, Marie-Jeanne, and the littlest, Sylvaine, were listening in. At first Marie-Jeanne thought there was a ray of sun shining through the window and skipping along the plain wooden table and over the egg cozies.

The sounds of morning activity outside in the little town with its bright pastel-colored houses wafted up into the flat above the bakery. Old cart wheels creaked and rattled over the bumpy cobblestones. Every lane in Nyons was crooked and slanting. "Perfect preparation for life," Elsa had told Marie-Jeanne. "If you only ever walk along level paths, you'll lose your balance when life gives you a shove—and I promise it will."

From the riverside drifted the aromas of the Autrand oil press, which had been producing soft, velvety olive oil for twelve generations, and somewhere or other a dog barked in time to the short, sharp clangs of the bells of St. Vincent's.

The sunny glow was now dancing in time to the movements of the elder daughters—for example, when they got to their feet, flung back their heads, rolled bread into little balls, and flicked them surreptitiously at one another. The twinkle settled on the upper lip of Noëlle Raspail, the eldest, whereas it snuggled up to Martine Raspail's neck. It didn't touch Madeleine, Loulou, or little Sylvaine. It twinkled with a, um . . . twinkle? A glow?

It looks like that sparkle on Elsa's finger, Marie-Jeanne thought. Curious and extraordinarily exciting.

No one else at the table seemed to have noticed. The parents were discussing whether they should join in with the strike on May 24.

"I beg you, madame," the father said to his wife, "how does it help the people of Nyons to go without bread?"

Madame said, "Monsieur, it's about taking a stand."

"But I ask you again, madame: Whom does that stand help?"

"It helps our daughters, monsieur."

After that, their communication was limited to glances that Marie-Jeanne for one interpreted as meaning: "Not in front of the kids!"

She didn't have a clue what they were talking about. The student revolution in Paris was a fire on an alien planet. What she did know, however, was that Noëlle and Martine were fervent supporters of this "stand." It was a matter of whether girls should really be forced to wear dresses to school and whether all women should be emancipated.

Marie-Jeanne watched in fascination as the twinkle pulsated on Noëlle's lip as if it were breathing. Breathing like a star. Very slowly and gracefully.

"Hey, what are you looking at, buttonhead?" The eldest

daughter had stopped crumbling her croissant into her coffee.

"Your mouth is glowing so beautifully, Noëlle. Like a star no one can take their eyes off."

"Ooh, aren't you dishing out the compliments!" Noëlle rolled her eyes. She had snarkiness down to a fine art. She dunked her soft golden pastry into her coffee again, and the twinkle pirouetted elegantly across her upper lip as she chewed.

When the Raspail parents left the kitchen, Noëlle leaned over to Martine. "*Dire non, c'est penser!* To say no is to think. We're going to the demo on the twenty-fourth, aren't we? Benoît's coming. And don't even think about snitching!"

"Dad won't let you go," Martine whispered back.

"He doesn't need to know, does he?"

Something was brewing.

Soon after breakfast Marie-Jeanne said goodbye, and she and Tictac ran through the narrow lanes, along small passageways between the brightly colored houses, and up the winding stairs to the fort and the Tour Randonne. She shot furtive glances at the mouth, hands, and neck of every woman she passed. Meanwhile, Tictac sniffed at other dogs' odorous calling cards and explored every nook and cranny. Cats observed his odd behavior but seemed to shrug it off.

That evening Marie-Jeanne studied Elsa's fingers as closely as she could. The fist alongside her plate, the fingers holding the napkin.

"Your hands are like the sun," she told her foster mother.

Elsa looked at Francis and furrowed her brow into creases

that reminded Marie-Jeanne of the stony ravines of the former mines in the valley around Condorcet.

"She's right," he said. "Like the sun in springtime, very early in the morning. The most beautiful sun there is."

"My word! Whatever did I do to deserve to live with a couple of comics like you, *porca miseria,*" Elsa mumbled, and her expression only accentuated the magnificence of her stony, wrinkled forehead.

Then suddenly, one morning, Loulou came to school with glowing hair.

8

A Slightly Peculiar Matter of the Greatest Significance

"What's that?" Marie-Jeanne asked as they lined up hand in hand outside the school gates.

"Where?"

"In your hair."

"Is it a bug or something? Take it out!"

"No. You're glowing brightly too."

"New shampoo," Loulou said with huge satisfaction.

"No chattering, *demoiselles*!"

They lowered their voices and Loulou said, almost inaudibly, "Hang on, what do you mean 'too'?"

"Well, like Noëlle and Martine."

"They're not *that* bright."

They both burst out giggling.

"Quiet now, Claudel and Raspail."

Marie-Jeanne naturally went out that same evening to 10,000 Articles, the new department store on Place des Arcades, to buy a bottle of this amazing product. She rubbed the suds into the tail of Josephine the donkey behind Francis's barn. Once, then a second time.

The courageous donkey was indulgent and held still. There was no glow. She washed her own hair. No glow.

Loud shouts from Elsa, much muttering from Francis. What was going on? Saturday was washday, not during the week!

It was all very curious, but maybe it was the "diplomacy" Francis had mentioned—the fact that everyone had their own truth?

Loulou's glow also behaved curiously whenever she came across the mayor's son on the school playground. Girls and boys mingled in the shade of the plane tree under supervision after a hard morning of lessons and a three-course school lunch (which they ate in silence, sitting bolt upright).

Luca. He had brown eyes brimming with summer and wild black hair, and he was far too clever to believe everything he was told by people in authority.

Loulou and Luca. When they stood next to each other they were complete. That, in any case, was how it looked to Marie-Jeanne. Pitch-black hair versus locks the color of brioche. One pair of brown eyes, the other green. They were the thunder and lightning of an approaching storm.

The two of them were constantly at loggerheads. Luca would shove her, Loulou would pinch him back, and then he would pull her hair (oh, how the glow spilled over then!). She thumped him, he called her names, and she hurled things at him. They were rivals in every respect at school—for the biggest mouth, the quickest at arithmetic, the worst marks and the best. They couldn't stand each other, or so it seemed.

When Marie-Jeanne asked Loulou if she might not actually fancy Luca, her friend slapped her and screamed, "Even if he were the last boy on earth, I'd rather see humanity die out than kiss him!"

"Of course," Marie-Jeanne lied.

"Why have you got that stupid grin on your face? Don't you believe me?"

"Oh, Loulou," Marie-Jeanne said, spreading her arms wide. Loulou threw herself into her embrace. She wept angry, bitter tears and sniffed.

"I don't know why . . . I don't know why I keep looking at him. He's such a moron. I hate him! Honestly. Does your cheek hurt, Marie?"

Even with the best will in the world, Marie-Jeanne couldn't answer her friend's first question, except for the fact that Luca's hands glowed when he teased Loulou. The second query, about her cheek, was easier to deal with: Her cheek was still smarting.

"Why do you keep going on about glowing?"

"What do you mean? I can't help it if people glow."

"And which part of Luca glows, did you say?"

"His hands. They glow twice as brightly when he pinches you."

"I reckon you made that up just to make me feel better."

Loulou gave Marie-Jeanne a big hug of her own and the next day she presented her friend with her favorite egg cozy.

It's incredible, Marie-Jeanne thought. *I deliberately don't lie and even then no one believes me.*

Clearly no one found the glowing especially remarkable, and so Marie-Jeanne decided to investigate. Now when she went to market with Elsa to help her *maman* sell her lace tablecloths, fans, bridal veils, and smart collars, the girl would screw up her eyes and observe events.

Meanwhile, her foster father planned the most astonishing enterprise of his life; Elsa made lace and cursed; the three homeless kittens Meeny, Miny, and Moe grew into cats; France set about reinventing itself; and Loulou and Luca dunked each other underwater in the river Eygues (until Loulou cried and Luca got so scared that he no longer dared approach her, putting a new expression on her face—a gentle hardening of the forehead). Now Loulou and Luca merely stared at each other from opposite sides of the playground and each averted their eyes whenever the other glanced in their direction.

If I were a song, I'd be one that can only be sung as a duet. If either singer falls silent, so do I.

Marie-Jeanne gradually realized that the twinkle was rarely seen on children, somewhat more frequently on bigger children like Loulou, and always on very big children like Martine and Noëlle, who already passed for adults. It was the size of a twenty-centime coin. On many people it was located around the level of the fourth shirt button, and it appeared earlier on girls than it did on boys.

Women took no notice of it, and very often the glow was to be found not on someone's shirt but on their fingers, mouth, or shoulders.

Loulou systematically claimed she couldn't see it, especially as she didn't care about Luca. Not a bit. She kept saying that too. "Not a bit, Marie. I can't even be bothered to ignore him."

. . .

So with whom could she talk about it?

How about Elsa? But she would tap Marie-Jeanne behind the ear with a wooden spoon and Francis would mumble into his sweater. This left her with only one option—the honorable priest.

"Hello, Father," Marie-Jeanne said when she came across him praying in the church. (Well, actually, he was merely kneeling there because he had been suffering from a slipped disc for years, and besides, a man could only think properly on his knees—about shopping, the weather, and the occasional wave of political upheaval in faraway Paris. It was also a pleasant position for digesting and kept visitors away outside working hours. And it was nice because it made him feel somehow at one with himself and the world.)

"Hello, my daughter," the priest answered reluctantly.

"You knew my mother?" Marie-Jeanne asked.

"What?"

"What do you mean, 'what'? Shouldn't that be 'who'?"

". . ."

"Anyway, hello. I have a slightly curious question of the utmost significance and no one to discuss it with."

Oh my goodness, thought the priest. *A precocious girl who only ever comes to church at Christmas. This could be tricky.*

"What can I do for you?" he asked sternly.

"I'd like to know . . . what this glowing means."

"Glowing? You mean the heavenly light? Or an epiphany? Haloes?"

"I don't know. Do you see the heavenly light on people's shoulders or mouths? In any case, it's never around the back and down below, so that might mean it is a heavenly light. It could hardly be . . . Sorry, what were all those names you listed?"

After a little toing and froing and a rapid description of the events in the Old and New Testaments, interrupted by skeptical questions from Marie-Jeanne ("But all she did was eat an apple!") that the priest found increasingly irritating, he decided that humans were generally incapable of seeing the heavenly light of the epiphany, least of all a girl on the verge of her eleventh birthday.

Naturally Marie-Jeanne wasn't satisfied. She shut her eyes. Anger was alien to her. Through closed eyelids she discerned the priest's despairing expression. It was rugged and beautiful in its desperation, which was both sincere and sad.

She opened her eyes and said gently and—she hoped—as diplomatically as possible, "You've been a great help."

His coin-sized glow was, incidentally, on his knees. Both knees! She'd never seen it there before. The glow flickered violently as he kneeled down again in relief and could sink back into quiet contemplation.

Marie-Jeanne decided not to tell him about the fabulous twinkling under his knees, because what would he have made of a halo floating around his legs?

I've already said that love comes in thousands of different guises, and a love of God—or rather, of oneself as an image of a pious person—is clearly one such guise.

9

The Top-secret Secret in a Love Letter

The revolution passed, summer came, the cicadas sang, the Pontias wind blew, and the second half of 1968 ticked away.

Francis made a few inquiries at the printer's in Grignan, and after a small glass of rosé at Luc le Marseillais's bar to get his courage up, he headed straight for Monsieur Mussigmann's bookshop. There he learned that more and more books were being published. *Those odd publishers in that strange far-off Paris must have their reasons for producing more and more books,* he thought. Those damn *Parigots* might have been a little off their rocker, but one thing was certain—they knew a thing or two about the future.

His conclusion was: *I'm going to step through this door. What have I got to lose?* (To which the answer was: nothing right now. Which was better than nothing at all.)

Before he actually opened that door, though, he wanted to hear what other people had to say. The first was an incredible lady called Madame Colette Brillant, to whose *mazet* in the folds of the hills around Condorcet he delivered vanloads of Sévigné paper, ink, quills, blotting paper, peculiar charcoal pencils, and small lengths of wood for picture frames from the Papeterie R. Begou & E. Pinet in Nyons.

Francis marveled each time at how bright it was inside her tidy house. He was only in a position to marvel because of Louis the Third's dogged, all-powerful engine. Soon after the Church of St. Peter and St. Paul, a chalky track called the rue du Vieux Village branched off the D70 and wound its way steeply uphill before petering out just beyond a vineyard at Madame Brillant's house. There was always at least one window open, and the breeze ruffled the curtains.

Outside the *mazet* a fig tree, an oak, a cedar, and an olive tree spread their shade, and at the back rosemary and lemon-scented sage flowered alongside stone steps made of worn, uneven lumps of rock. Thyme and chives twitched in the rippling wind.

The view from here took in the whole valley of the Angèle massif, which was shaped like a woman lying on her side. People said that there were no brighter, more peaceful, or more forgotten slopes in the whole of the Baronnies. That might have been true, but what was more important was that Madame Brillant could see the white cap of Mont Ventoux. On certain days, when the mist hung low, the color drained from the mountain ranges and they looked like something out of a dream.

Once, when Francis asked her why she had left Montélimar, she had replied, "I wanted to learn to see again."

Colette Brillant was a calligrapher and had produced official documents for the Orange city council. Not certificates for stupid sports days where young people are humiliated by being forced to perform a series of pointless exercises with their lanky limbs. No. Commendations, certificates for partner towns, entries into the city's gilt-edged archive books, that kind of thing.

She was also a graphologist: She analyzed people's handwriting. She also painted, read people's hands and ears—"You have the ears of a conqueror, my dear Francis." "Oh really? My father said I had his uncle's ears, but he never got farther than Chaudebonne." She knew exactly which of the stones she had collected up at the ruins could be split with a hammer to reveal a fossil, and she had books everywhere, even in her kitchen.

Of course, the kitchen was also the dining room, the living room, and her study (in the form of a slightly skewed tabletop). A steep wooden staircase next to the fireplace led up to the attic, where Francis guessed she must have her bedroom and washstand.

Madame Brillant occasionally asked Francis to chop some firewood for her and pile it up in her tiny shed. While he was doing this, she would take the opportunity to teach Marie-Jeanne a thing or two in return for Francis's efforts. Well, from time to time he was rewarded with a tasty helping of potato stew with olives, fresh garlic, olive oil, and whole bunches of rosemary from her hillside garden at an outside table with tall candles flickering in wide-jawed jars and wine that diffracted the sun's rays. Francis hadn't known it was possible to have such a festive time in midweek, other than on public holidays.

He couldn't know that Colette Brillant forced herself to celebrate her loneliness to avoid sinking into complete emptiness. The idea that she would never love again pained her, which is why she focused on making her life as nice as possible.

What Madame Colette Brillant didn't say

Colette had lived for two decades with a man who had come between her and her book every night. On the whole he didn't appreciate women who read too much and who preferred their own company to his. He was inconsiderate and always hungry for attention, his desperation like a permanent black hole. However much someone filled it, he was never satisfied, only spiteful.

She hurled everything she had into the maw of the involuntary upstart (he probably wasn't happy with himself either) and hurled herself to the ground, but he would actually have preferred it to open up and swallow her so he could take up the space he needed—every last inch of space.

Since Colette wouldn't do him this favor and insisted on living her own life, come what may, he burned her books in the fireplace, laughing as they went up in smoke. Dickens, Chekhov, Lindgren, du Maurier, Nin, Joyce. Every single one.

"See how much I love you, Colette. I can't even bear to have that Miller of yours or that bloke Kant as a rival."

It was barbaric.

I was standing next to her at the time, cradling her heart in my hands as it refused to break. Next to me were Passion and Fear. They'd once paid her a premature visit, and so—out of passion and, yes, out of fear that she wouldn't take anyone else, and yes, because she felt responsible for the amorous Narcissus's suffering—she said yes to this man. He was good for no one, not even for himself.

Passion and Fear looked at the burning books, and even they felt humbled.

So Colette left Montélimar to find out what it was like to pick herself up and live alone with her books and no one else. But still she hungered to mean the world to someone else, someone who saw this world the same way she did; someone who loved it and welcomed its possibilities as she did. Madame Colette Brillant deserved her name: She was brilliant.

Like me, she loved food, but cooking . . . not so much. She still thought back with nostalgia and delight to a job she had done, what was it . . . ten years ago? She had designed the menus for a restaurant in Sanary-sur-Mer. The dishes had appeared in her mind's eye, each composition telling a wonderful, intimate story of those southern climes, the invisible life of the sea, and the man who had prepared these offerings with serenity and dignity. She would have loved to try them all. With someone sitting opposite her, watching. A dinner partner smiling at her. With a man who made her feel safe.

I knew the right man, but as long as Colette remained here in the mountains, her freedom only expressed in calligraphy on handmade paper, and this gentleman stared out to sea every night, not knowing whether the quiet pain inside him was real or simply the chill nighttime breeze, I could do nothing for her. I could only watch, wait, and hope. I wouldn't wish such a hellish ordeal on anyone.

Meanwhile, standing there, his eyes hurting from the sight of petrified waves of hills and mountains, montagne de Sigala and Autuche, Ambonne and Angèle, Francis could understand why one might wish to "learn to see again."

What was it dreamers said? Sometimes you had to reach for the stars to touch the sky.

Marie-Jeanne loved accompanying Francis to Madame Colette's. She loved the sound of the wind and the bees and the short, sharp chimes of Peter and Paul in Condorcet, and she was even more excited about visiting the cemetery in the old village center with its half-sunken gravestones and bright, perennial plastic flowers. Francis told her to whistle at regular intervals as it might be dangerous up there on the escarpment. The slope suddenly fell away on the other side of the hill as if the nose had been cut off a huge chunk of cheese, and the place was teeming with wild boar that could effortlessly trample a little girl to a pulp.

Colette had plans to expand Marie-Jeanne's knowledge beyond the mountaintops. One thing was to ensure that she could write legibly. She had Marie-Jeanne copy out a poem from a book she'd plucked thoughtfully from a bookcase.

The minute I heard my first love story,
I started looking for you, not knowing
how blind that was.
Lovers don't finally meet somewhere.
They're in each other all along.

"That's lovely. Who wrote it?"

"Rumi. Hardly any other words are so profoundly rooted

in the beauty of calligraphy as his lines about love. Wouldn't it be marvelous if they were true?"

Colette studied Marie-Jeanne's scratchy attempts at writing.

"You don't write decisively enough. Look, part of you is in every bit of handwriting you do. Writing expresses your personality, my girl, and yours is a work in progress. It doesn't have to decide on its future path just yet."

"Will it always be like that?"

"Handwriting never stays the same. It's a reflection of your life. Our handwriting suffers with us. Lovers write differently from the brokenhearted, mourners differently from those who haven't been hurt, the seduced differently from seducers."

"What are seducers?"

"People who can persuade you to do what you want to do but have, for intelligent or stupid reasons, denied yourself. What matters is being able to tell the difference at the right time."

Colette reached for one of her ink drawings of the Chinese character for "freedom."

"Your breathing is also visible in your handwriting. Take this for example. The character for 'freedom' is a complex combination of two characters—the 'self,' represented by the symbol for 'breath,' and 'sprouting grain,' which stands for 'one's own realm.' It's good to breathe in and out deeply whenever you have a tough decision to make. You'll usually find the appropriate solution by breathing out. It doesn't have to be the correct or the most reasonable solution, just your own. See the difference? You can always decide to do something that isn't sensible purely because you are free to do so."

Marie-Jeanne nodded very slowly and earnestly.

Francis had quietly joined them and was listening in silence. It was strange, what words could do. Had he ever registered his breathing?

Marie-Jeanne found something that made her head spin in a book about Farsi script in Colette Brillant's library.

" 'According to a Persian legend, someone who writes their name on a piece of paper and presents it to another person has given away the most important thread of their soul. This leash consisting of ink, devotion, and humility can be used to call them and lead them around until the owner of the written name returns the piece of paper, destroys it, or removes it from their home,' " she read out.

(I can confirm this—another of those miracles for which none of us wishes to be held responsible.)

"It used to be said that you should never sign your full name at the end of a handwritten letter if you aren't completely sure you are willing to belong to the recipient," Colette added. "That's especially true of love letters."

"I'll take note," Marie-Jeanne muttered.

"Have you ever received a love letter?"

"No!"

"Or written one?"

"No, I wouldn't know how or to whom."

"That must put your parents' minds at ease."

There was a cough from the doorway. "And you find all these things in . . . books?" Francis asked.

10

Books Are Not for Cowards

Those words about love, and being in each other all along, had set something humming inside Francis. *Elsa,* he thought. *My Elsa.* He considered what he had heard about the piece of paper and the name written on it. He'd never written Elsa a love letter. There was no chance that she would ever write him one, but *he* could give it a go. It wouldn't take more than a few months. He could have it done by Christmas. How on earth did the people who wrote these things know about them? And what else was there in books that he, Francis, a bric-a-brac dealer in the remotest part of France, didn't know? It made him eager to learn more about things that, to his surprise, made life more . . . complete. Like that stuff about sensible decisions and your own decisions. Once you started on these books, could you ever get enough?

"Wouldn't you like to take a look at the vineyard, Marie?" he asked.

"No way," said the moody child, pretending not to have understood that the adults wanted to discuss grown-up matters.

Francis sighed. "Um, about these books," he said, waving

his hand vaguely in the direction of the slightly bowed wooden planks with dozens of books piled on top of them.

Lessing, Camus, Duras, Adorno, Sagan. Oh look, she had some Barjavel too. Joyce, Eliot, Sand. Miller, du Maurier. Seneca, Hugo, Colette. And others with unpronounceable names: Maugham, Fitzgerald, Salinger, Huxley, Woolf.

He looked at his foster daughter again and cleared his throat.

"Okay, I get it." She slipped outside—not too quickly, of course—to go and stop Tictac from chasing Madame Colette's comical white chickens around the cedar.

"You're wondering if I've read them all?"

"I'm assuming they aren't just there for decorative purposes."

Colette laughed. "Oh, some people do decorate their lives with books to impress other fools. To misinterpret them as a badge of superiority is an insult to books. Books are nothing to feel smug about. They're constantly reining in our arrogance."

Francis contemplated this statement. Unfortunately he quickly came to the conclusion that he was himself precisely such a fool. In any case, the apparent cultivation of Monsieur Mussigmann, the bookseller in Nyons, intimidated him and made him feel supremely dumb in comparison, from the parting in his home-cut hair down to the worn-out soles of his shoes. The clothes he wore, how he greeted people, the way he stood there in embarrassment with his hands in his pockets, gawping at these unfamiliar paper objects deep inside which he suspected there must be monsters, astounding truths, and descriptions of feelings he would probably never have.

"Do you know who consoles me when I feel small?"

"It would be quite surprising if I did, madame."

Colette laughed and swiftly reached for a dog-eared book on the shelf.

"Seneca. He was an adviser to the Roman emperor Caligula. There are doubts as to whether his advice had any effect. 'For the soul is more powerful than any sort of fortune.' " She leafed through the book. "Listen to this. It's one of my favorite passages. 'Who of these would not rather have the state disordered than his hair? Who is not more concerned to have his head trimmed rather than safe? Who would not rather be well barbered than upright?' "

"I know some people like that," said Francis.

"See, Seneca and you are less different than you might think."

"But books can be so thick and the sentences so long that by the time I get to the end I've forgotten how they started."

She gave a mischievous laugh. "You know, books teach us many things, including persistence. Here"—she pulled out Thomas Mann's *The Magic Mountain*—"you get the feeling that some of the sentences in this book last longer than a lifetime. Try holding your breath as you read one of these monsters. After you've made it through Thomas Mann or this, *Robinson Crusoe,* no other challenge in life will seem quite so daunting. Anyway, what was it you wanted to discuss?"

Relieved, Francis presented the thoughts that had triggered the *ding-ding* in his head. Quietly, so the idea wasn't ruined.

At first Colette arched her eyebrows—both of them, not a great sign!—but first one and then the other came down and the corners of her mouth curled upward.

"Ha!" she cried. "Your heart is rebelling. Good!"

She swung around and once more plunged her ink-stained

hand unwaveringly into the shelf. She flicked through her chosen book, searching for the passage she wanted, and then launched into a very long and very fast speech, which I have attempted to summarize as follows.

From an obscure myth

Thoth was something like a heavenly secretary to the god Osiris. Legend has it that he invented language, but his power was largely based on the belief that he also invented magic. That's because no spell works without language (can you imagine a sorceress without her book of magic spells?), and once you've realized that, you also know that it is only through language, literature, and poetry that things come to life. They endow objects with a smell and a shape, meaning and form. Books are the fount of all creation, not some accidental by-product.

That, at any rate, was how Colette saw things. "Life was created because someone described it. Love was born when someone sang it into life. Humankind arose because someone put pen to paper and wrote: 'Once upon a time there was a man . . .'"

"Aha," went Francis.

Viewed in these terms, books were the last of the old magic. They made silent facts visible. They transformed their readers, metamorphosed them, opened doors into other people's heads and the bodies of strangers, even when they'd been dead for hundreds of years. Readers explored someone else's mind, dreamed someone else's dreams, walked in a different body, felt what strangers felt in their misery and desperation and passion, traveled through different lands and parallel universes without moving. They suddenly became old or young again and slipped into a different gender or a different-colored skin.

"Hmm," Francis said.

Telepathy, astral projections, communicating with the dead in the underworld, or living on after your own death? Pff . . . no big deal. Just open a book!

Books turn people into time travelers, shape shifters, body switchers, mind readers, and immortals, and therefore books are the last great alchemy of our age.

They are very, very dangerous indeed.

"Wow," Francis said. He liked the prospect. Sort of.

Colette smiled. "Do you know what women of my age think of life?"

Francis gave a cough.

"I'm going to tell you. These days a woman can either become an anarchist or enter a convent."

"This doesn't look much like a convent."

"That's right," she said. "I'm all for it, Monsieur Meurienne. It's amazing there isn't already one around here. The more you think about it, the more obvious it seems. You are, in fact, an anarchist."

"I don't do much thinking," Francis said, turning red.

"Don't worry. Your plans will necessarily change that. You'll cause a lot of unrest around here. What did you say you wanted to call this thing?"

He repeated it, even more quietly.

When Marie-Jeanne returned with Tictac in tow, clearly delighted by his bad behavior, Madame Colette and Francis were hunched over a sheet of handmade paper. Marie-Jeanne couldn't make out what the lady was writing over and over again in a variety of styles, but after a while Francis nodded and said, "That's it."

That's when Marie-Jeanne noticed that the fingers of Madame Colette's right hand were glowing as if she had a little lamp on her fingertips.

Satisfied, Colette turned the piece of paper over before Marie-Jeanne could see what she'd written. What she would remember forever, however, were the calligrapher's words to her foster father.

"My dear Francis, books are not for cowards."

11

The Results of Marie-Jeanne Claudel's Study into the Nature of the Strange Illuminations on People's Bodies

"What?" Elsa snarled.

"Excuse me?!" she exclaimed.

"Why?" she asked.

"Because books aren't for cowards and I don't want to be a coward. I want something . . . well, I want to do something that . . . that changes the face of our time, you know. I don't want to go through life without changing anything. It isn't a sensible decision, but it's my own."

Elsa stared at her husband, mulled over all the stuff about the face of time, thought about her wrinkles, studied his boat-shaped mouth, and considered how he had once had a full head of hair and whether that had somehow altered his face over time and maybe not for the better. Finally, she understood what he had said.

He wanted . . . Well, she never . . . It was outrageous. That's right: Francis was going to mortgage everything—the house, the barn, their land. Not Marie-Jeanne's *mazet,* though. Even if it all went wrong, the girl would still have a roof over her head.

Elsa didn't speak to Francis for a fortnight.

He missed her grumbling and comments. It made him feel ill at ease and cold.

We can guess what had happened: Elsa was speechless. Her muttering and grimacing had ceased. This was, in fact, a token of her admiration for her husband's daring, pride, and plans, but I presume only Marie-Jeanne and I knew that.

Thank goodness the girl could never have disclosed *how* she knew it, not even if she'd been roasted over a wood fire like Elsa's delicious garlic bread. (She rubbed thick slices with velvety, summery, liquid-green olive oil and fresh, subtle, purple garlic before layering chopped beefsteak tomatoes on top and sprinkling them with sea salt. . . .)

Sorry about that, but I do love good food, and oddly enough, most of the greatest love stories are sustained by sharing tasty meals. Now, where were we? . . . Oh yes . . .

Marie-Jeanne interpreted her foster mother's silence as a sign of respect for Francis's boldness, yet simultaneously of her worry that he might become so successful that he no longer needed his fearsome wife.

Other questions were also bugging Elsa. What had gotten into him about these books? Was she supposed to start reading too? When would she fit it in, for goodness' sake?

You must allow me a moment's digression. You see, I'm still stunned by the fact that the fallout from Francis's madcap plan opened a doorway for his daughter into an invisible world.

Marie-Jeanne had seen Madame Brillant brimming with excitement about Francis's idea, her fingers glowing as they began carefully forming letters. She had seen the same glow on the baker's young daughters and the surly priest.

And now she spotted it on Elsa too—tiny sparks that twinkled a little more brightly every time she served her husband some food, *despite* her censorious silence.

In truth, it was her cooking that gave Elsa away. She baked her smile into her *brouillade,* a dish of scrambled eggs with local Rabasse black truffles. (Elsa and Tictac had a talent for finding truffles: Elsa would observe a particular type of gnat found only over truffle nests, and Tictac would confirm her premonition by excavating the soil or rolling lazily in the sun, depending.) When she fried zucchini flowers, she fanned the flames under the pan of salted butter with her pride in her husband. She stirred her affection into a risotto and a brace of filleted and gently grilled trout that Marie-Jeanne had caught. In a decidedly banal century, this forgotten culinary magic was her way of conveying her affection and smiles and pride. It made Francis feel calm and bright and warm inside.

Elsa longed to sneak up behind Francis; wrap her strong, warm, soft-skinned arms around him; and, in all her helpless, shining love, never let go of him again, but she couldn't quite bring herself to do it. It made for a vaguely amusing but agonizing spectacle. She was breaking her own heart, and that is the second-most terrible thing that Love can witness: a person who forbids herself to love.

Oh, Elsa.

Marie-Jeanne continued her investigations into the strange glow with the fierce determination of a young soul hell-bent on penetrating life's essential secrets. She noted down who glowed where, when, and how, and what caused this glow, and tried to ascertain the logic behind these sequences.

In some of the people Marie-Jeanne observed on the Nyons market square, the glow seemed faded and bruised. In her notebook she wrote: "Like cups that have been shattered and mended many times." In addition, it struck her that the mayor's dog, Rosso, lit up the large plane tree on the Place des Arcades. The olive tree told her that trees found it incredibly irritating when dogs got too excited about them, but they could do little in self-defense—with the exception of horse chestnuts, of course.

Marie-Jeanne, you see, began to see people as I do.

The results of Marie-Jeanne Claudel's study into the nature of the strange illuminations on people's bodies

The glowing did not distinguish between nice and not nice, between good and bad, beautiful and not beautiful. That seemed to rule out the notion of a halo. It was just as likely to affect the nasty cobbler as friendly Martine Raspail; it wasn't bothered by the mayor's triple chin or someone else's cleft lip.

Everyone over thirteen had it, which also excluded the idea of enlightenment, since the glow made them neither cleverer nor kinder. Rather the opposite, if anything. (Marie-Jeanne thought that this "opposite" probably deserved closer consideration. Loulou and Luca's behavior offered a dazzling illustration of this: They seemed to lose their wits, to put it mildly, whenever they ran into each other and acted like . . . like . . . Marie-Jeanne searched for a long time for a fitting word and eventually settled on "idiots.")

Every human was illuminated and so were dogs, which may have been attributable to the fact that they regard themselves as humans with fur. Cats didn't, though—as everyone knows, they regard themselves as gods. But cats *could* make the glow start to bubble, as when Meeny, Miny, and Moe clambered around on top of Elsa and she smiled like a chubbier version of that woman in that Parisian museum Marie-Jeanne had read about in art class—Mona Lisa, that was her name.

The glow could breathe, bubble, throb, laugh, smile, pump, and make sparks fly. In the absence of a more scientifically appropriate term, Marie-Jeanne decided to call this general symptom a "glow-purr." The purring was loudest when someone touched the relevant spot. It generally fizzed when people did something they enjoyed, for example when the dough Loulou's dad was kneading made funny farting noises.

She also noticed that the glow was never—absolutely never—"behind-and-below," as Elsa had told her to refer to that area of the body.

Loulou began to think that Marie-Jeanne might be a bit nuts when her friend started pointing this way and that, commenting, "Look, your mother has it on her left shoulder and your father's got one on his mouth, and if he kissed your mother on the shoulder . . ."

"He never does that kind of thing!"

"Why not?"

Loulou looked at her in amazement. "I don't know."

"Maybe he should try?"

"Do fathers really kiss mothers?"

They had a good think about this, but neither of them was really sure.

"Madame Châtelet has one on her forehead. You can't miss it!"

"I don't know where you get these ideas," Loulou said seriously, "but did you know that Géraldine Châtelet has a secret lover?"

"What's one of those?"

"No idea. Noëlle told me."

So they went off to find Loulou's sister, who took a little persuading before she would spill the beans. She reported the following: Madame Géraldine Châtelet, a solicitor, had never married and lived alone, only very rarely accepting invitations and disappearing off to Aix or Orange or Arles or even—whisper it—Marseille in her magnificent dark blue Citroën DS on the weekends. She had dropped a hint that she danced Argentine tango.

But—and this was the clincher—Noëlle, who, like the other two elder sisters, helped out in the bakery, mostly in the evenings, could report that Madame Châtelet often bought baguettes—always Tradition or Campagnarde—for two. At the market on Thursdays she also shopped for two, even though she didn't look like someone with the appetite of two people. Did she have a secret lover?

"What's a lover?" asked Marie-Jeanne.

"Someone who loves someone," Loulou answered, imitating her big sister's eye-roll.

But it was the word "secret" that put Loulou in a tizzy.

Doing something secretly meant sipping at the springs of joy and experiencing the exquisite fear of discovery.

They immediately decided to spy on Madame Châtelet. Or rather, Loulou decided to spy on her. She needed something to distract her now that horrible Luca no longer did.

Marie-Jeanne was swept along by Loulou's enthusiasm for this plan. Maybe, just maybe, her friend would finally spot the glow. However, she was also curious because Madame Châtelet's glow flickered only faintly.

So when Madame Châtelet left her flat to pick up her usual twin baguettes, the two well-meaning rascals sneaked into her flat and hid in the hallway cupboard, the one with small openings covered with fly nets. The cupboard smelled of lavender. From it they had an excellent view of the living room, with its pretty dining table, armchairs, and gramophone, and the open kitchen beyond.

The living room gave onto a tiny roof terrace covered with a wood and raffia roof, furnished with oriental trays and glasses and occupied by an arrogant, sharp-featured white cat that sprawled proprietorially on the warm tiles, keeping an eye on goings-on on rue du Pontias below.

"My foot's gone numb," said Loulou.

"I think the cat knows we're here."

"She won't tell on us, though."

"Are you sure?"

"I need to pee."

"Me too."

They clasped each other's hands. There was no going back now.

12

The Translucent Wings of the Heart

Géraldine Châtelet came home soon afterward.

"I'm home," she cried in a high-pitched girly voice, laying the two baguettes on a large wooden board that looked as if generations of solicitors had cut bread on it.

"Fix yourself a drink, darling. I'll be right with you."

Darling? Loulou mouthed in the cupboard. Was Madame Châtelet talking to her white cat?

The solicitor hummed as she made her way to her bedroom and reappeared completely transformed. She'd swapped her elegant but slightly stuffy suit for a beautiful blue dress, decorated with a yellow-and-red flowery pattern, that swirled around her knees with every step.

Soon tango music started to play, or what Marie-Jeanne imagined must be tango music because she'd never heard anything like it before. Bandoneon, violins, an incredible rhythm.

"To us!" Madame Châtelet was saying, and the two girls caught sight of her holding a tall, slender champagne glass in each hand and clinking them together. There was the sound of glass on glass. She smiled. She looked both absolutely gorgeous and awfully sad.

A scourge of even experienced men because she wouldn't put up with bad behavior (which ranged from inappropriate jokes to inappropriate cheerfulness), Madame Châtelet set the table for two, lit some candles, chatted with her imaginary guest, cooked, and served wine (only for herself). In the cupboard Loulou and Marie-Jeanne held hands even more tightly.

Maybe this wasn't such a good idea. They both felt ashamed. Ashamed that madame was so absorbed in her beautiful, sad delusion and completely oblivious to her stupid witnesses.

Next Madame Châtelet read aloud from a book by a woman called Simone Weil with eloquence and intelligence, but the girls didn't understand a word. Next, she opened a notebook. She leafed through it. She sighed. She took a sip of wine, flicked through the pages, and finally read something out loud.

Sometimes a voice thunders inside me.
Sometimes it merely whispers.
Sometimes it is silent
and then
I lie quietly and decorate the cage
of sensible reasons
and watch the wildness of the love within.
The fabric of dreams and memories.
I drape myself in the journeys
I've undertaken inside you.
You are so fine, so
distant,
and so I live on and laugh
the laughter that was meant for you.

Slowly she closed the notebook.

"That was a long time ago," she announced to the empty room. "I loved a man and he loved me. We were never together. We never drank a single kiss from each other's lips, not one. Sensible reasons . . . another family . . . honor and loyalty. A promise."

She took another sip.

"We wrote each other letters. So many letters. Writing to him was like kissing him, and I felt like writing him a thousand letters. But happiness cannot be gained for the price of unhappiness. What should I have done differently? He made me happy, and I him. So my only option was to stay away from him before we hurt people who also loved him and needed him. I wish I'd never been so happy with that . . . that beast, or I wouldn't miss him so much. Then I wouldn't have died so often of despair from knowing how it felt to be whole, to be complete. Happiness. I wish I hadn't been happy."

She drained her wine in one swig.

"He only loved me in his thoughts. Useless thoughts!"

She hurled the glass against the wall.

"What a wasted life! What wasted love! What cruelty! Such damn cruel love! It ought to have left us alone. People who aren't free shouldn't be allowed to fall in love with each other. They should never be allowed to meet. Now, that would be fair, do you hear me? That would be fair!"

I stood there with my back against the wall, close to the two girls, with my head bowed. Yes, that was how it ought to be, but it seldom was. Fate didn't pretend to be fair.

. . .

Now the temperature of the one-sided conversation changed.

"I miss you so," Géraldine Châtelet whispered. "I have so much to tell you. I'd love to live again. I'd love to go dancing, with you, and even if you only watched, that would be fine. I'd love to argue with you. About Weil and Foucault and all the rest . . . All the rest. But look how time has swallowed me. Will you let me depart without having ever truly loved a man?"

She buried her face in her hands and wept silently as the candlelight flickered on the beautifully laid table. As the music played. As the two glasses stood there and only one was sipped.

"Where are you? Do you even exist for me?"

Grabbing a plate, she smashed it on the floor.

"You've betrayed me!" she whispered. A low, despairing whisper.

"Who betrayed her? The man she no longer laughs for?" hissed Loulou.

"Or a man she loves but doesn't know?"

I could have told them that Géraldine was talking about me. She thought that I'd betrayed her and forced her to endure many days when she felt so helpless that she could barely breathe, when every day and every night were haunted by an elusive name. I couldn't break off the relationship. All I could do was to touch her a second time, inspire a new relationship, and request graciously and humbly that Fate do its bit. I could have murdered Fate, though. How could it tie one of two lovers down so tightly that their love stood no chance—no chance if that person was an upstanding man who refused to inflict terrible pain on his family in exchange for his own selfish happiness.

"Marie? What do you think—"

"Who's there?" Géraldine Châtelet said suddenly in her solicitor's voice, utterly transformed.

The girls tried to shrink farther back into the cupboard, although tragically that wasn't possible, unless they were to metamorphose into tiny clothes moths.

It didn't take her long to find them. First she stared at her feet in shame before slapping both girls—one, two!—on each cheek, then she grabbed a broom and swept them out of the flat.

"You'd better not tell anyone!" she warned them quietly with a mixture of rage, despair, imploring, and highhandedness.

The two girls rapidly nodded with relief, fear, sheepishness, sympathy, and shock. All three of them knew they would never mention what had happened.

The girls walked hand in hand through Nyons without a word until their palms began to sweat.

"Marie? Can you still see the broom?" Loulou asked after a while, glancing over her shoulder and pointing to her behind-and-below.

Her friend shook her head.

"What if we turn out like Madame Châtelet?"

"What do you mean, Lou?"

"You know, grown-up and sad and alone because we love someone who doesn't love us back. Or he does love us, but it's impossible. Or we can't find him, ever. Or we're happy for only a short time and then never as much again. Have you ever thought of that?"

Marie-Jeanne shrugged. "We'll have dinner together. Us two, you and me, with our invisible old lovers. All four of us. And if we stay single, we'll live together, I swear."

They held hands and walked on, parting only when they reached the Roman bridge by the olive mill. As she watched Loulou run back to the bakery, she saw that the five haloes in her friend's hair had shrunk to little circles now, dull and pale.

Yet Marie-Jeanne couldn't really ask Luca to play more of his mean tricks that had always set off fireworks in Loulou's head. She came to the conclusion that Loulou had unexpectedly come of age that evening. It was as if she'd become aware of the end of childhood and the dawn of a very grown-up despair at losing something before she'd even found it. And Loulou had lost all hope of a better tomorrow.

She wondered why love was so heavy. Wasn't it supposed to make you feel as weightless as if you were made of light?

13

Francis Meurienne's Mobile Library

In the autumn of 1968, half a year after the *ding-ding* in Francis's head, Louis the Third acquired two siblings: Louis the Fourth and Louis the Fifth, both blue 2CV vans like their elder brother. Emblazoned across their side doors in Madame Colette Brillant's lettering were the words:

Philis Mobile Library
Literary loans and orders

"Tada!" said Francis.

"Dear me," Elsa muttered.

The Philis Mobile Library, named after the belligerent, literature-and-freedom-loving defender of the Dauphiné, had fixed lunchtime stops on market days in the region's larger towns—Nyons on Thursdays, Buis-les-Baronnies on Wednesdays, Mirabel on Fridays, Sauzet on Saturdays, and Taulignan on Sundays. In the afternoons and on the remaining days of the week, it would tour isolated villages and farms to offer doorstop borrowing and pick up previous loans.

Francis would refer orders and purchases to Monsieur Mussigmann in Nyons, and they would split a small commission between them. The bookseller's role was to order discount copies from publishing houses. Together Francis and Monsieur Mussigmann would pay 6 percent of the purchase price into the authors' social security fund.

Some people needed books but couldn't afford them or couldn't make it to the nearest library in Montélimar, where no one ever went. In such circumstances, there was a good case to be made for everyone to pool them—for a modest loan fee.

That had been Francis's original plan. But frightful Fate made things a little more complicated than that. Of course it did.

Francis Meurienne's mobile library. The valley between the four mountains hadn't seen anything this strange, unprecedented, and surprising in a very long time, probably since the day Olga the five-legged dog was born. People would have been no less stunned if Francis had opened a shop selling giraffes.

When Francis presented his idea to the mayors of the various towns, he was met with, let's say, a good measure of reticence. The administrators—generally the sole baker, cheesemaker, or blacksmith in the place, who carried out their mayoral duties from a counter decked out with the French flag next to the bakehouse, cheese display, or smithy—remained unconvinced.

"Listen, Francis, these aren't textbooks, and anyway, we always buy those in August."

"But these aren't textbooks for school anyway."

"They aren't?"

"No, they're textbooks for life."

They would examine the books suspiciously with the tips of their fingers. "*The Catcher in the Rye.* What on earth is this supposed to teach anyone? We don't grow rye around here."

"I guess everyone learns something different from a book."

Two men in the prime of their lives sized up Francis disdainfully. "People who read don't work, Francis!"

"But someone who reads will come up with new ideas and be equipped for a changing world."

"Oh yeah? Like that lad in the rye? Listen, Francis, just because something's new, it doesn't automatically make it better."

Much head-shaking and crossing of arms. Meeting over. He would drive home having achieved nothing.

He made the other promotional tours to the farms in the four hills with Josephine, a.k.a. Fino, meeting all kinds of characters who usually passed their time in the company of goats, the wind, cheese, and the unfolding seasons. He spent the first few weeks unsuccessfully trying to persuade them that books posed no danger whatsoever to their daughters' virtue, as everyone claimed.

The crux of his argument was this: "You don't want to be left behind, do you?"

Should one of these old people continue to fight tooth and nail and with furrowed brow against books' entering his home, one of precisely three conversations would ensue.

The most frequent response was: "Listen here, Francis. If she reads, she'll become too clever by half."

"Too clever for what?"

"You know, for everything. Finding a husband, doing the housework . . . She'll answer back in words I don't understand, you see? I bet all of those crazy young students in Paris last May were readers, and look where that led. Nothing's the way it used to be."

"The old days weren't always better, you know." A silence, followed by more gentle probing from Francis. "You could read something and give her a decent idea of the contents."

"You seriously think I've got time?"

"Maybe on the toilet?"

"I read comics there."

"I get the feeling you may not be a true Occitan, Bobo. You know, this used to be the cradle of culture and freedom and—"

"Good God, Francis! Okay, give it to me then, but if it contains any smut, I swear I'll shoot you."

The second-most frequent was: "Listen, Francis, you can't just plant a seed in any old soil. Books and my daughters just don't go together. You don't plant a lemon tree on the Champs-Élysées."

"Unlike lemon trees, though, your girls have feet to take them wherever they like, Maurice."

"I'm sorry, but what would they do there?"

"Be happy, maybe?"

"What a strange idea! Did we come into this world to be happy?"

The third-most common dialogue went as follows:

"Listen, Francis, who's supposed to put up with all the dissatisfied women?"

"Why would they be dissatisfied, Laurent?"

"Because they've read all that stuff and want all that stuff—I don't know, cars and villas in Cannes—and they'll all head off to Paris. They look around and see what's going on here—nothing worth putting in a book. And then how am I meant to pay for it, eh?"

Francis came up with a range of strategies. He imagined that most of the men were simply embarrassed. Most of them had left school at eleven having read *The Little Prince* and been forced to learn some Greek mythology and study the first few pages of the *Dictionnaire Larousse*. After that, they had done an apprenticeship or immediately returned to their farms, their only outings a trip to the cinema every few months. The purchase of a telephone and the later acquisition of a television set had caused family upheaval similar to a rerun of the revolution.

Their farms, Nyons, the tracks and roads between the two, and perhaps a twenty- or thirty-mile radius: That was their world. Then there were the rules that governed this world. Celebrating public holidays, holding marriages, tending graves. Children accepting punishments without protest, and parents dealing them out on a regular basis. A widespread distrust of education, as if it dulled critical areas of people's brains and caused them to forget the basic principles of life. These basic principles were: not getting too big for your boots, knowing in which phase of the moon to sow your fields, never wasting bread, being able to grind coffee beans properly, knowing where you belonged, standing by the side of the road when the Tour de France sped past, commemorating the war, and remembering that things were good as they were and should not be jeopardized.

Anywhere else, even the next *département*—Alpes de Haute Provence, Ardèche, or Isère—was no more than a vague notion, far away even now as a new age dawned in the wake of May '68. Different people lived there, with different customs. Who knows: Maybe they even lived in a completely different time? The sense of identity here in this forgotten valley people passed through on the N7 as they motored south to the Mediterranean beaches stretched no farther than one hour's drive in any direction. And now, all of a sudden, books were going to march into this world, bringing thousands of other worlds with them? Maybe they'd usher in the new era on everyone's lips. Even the restless youth of this forgotten valley discussed it more and more openly.

Youngsters were always grumbling. They wanted bikinis and portable radios. They wanted to pass their driving test. They wanted to address their parents by their first names rather than by the formal *vous*. They wanted to read *Lui* magazine and play Jacques Dutronc at full volume and give their mother a Moulinex for Christmas because "Moulinex liberates women."

"Aha," said Francis.

And the farmers concluded, "Look what trouble the extension of the school-going age in 1966 caused hardworking fathers."

Also, what if fathers and grandfathers didn't understand these books?

They didn't really say that. What they said was: What if literature turned their daughters, whom they had tried so hard to raise into upstanding women, into the butt of neighborly gossip?

In fact, their nearest neighbors lived three miles away, but still . . . Rumors were cooked up under the arcades and plane trees of the Nyons market square, and then spread from stall to stall, over live chickens and across displays of goat cheeses, passed on with barrels of olives, and eventually a daughter wouldn't find a husband simply because she'd stuck her nose into the wrong book. Or worse, the lass would say, "Why would I need a husband?" What then?

It would stir up trouble too. First with the wife, then with your buddies, and all the rest . . . Reputation was important—the smaller the world, the more indispensable—and if Francis didn't accept that, then he was . . .

"That's absurd," Francis said. "No young man ever stopped desiring a woman just because she read books. What's more, reading will lower the risk of her lumbering herself with a good-for-nothing. Anyway, don't you think it's odd that none of this crosses your mind when you think about your sons' reputations?"

"Pssh! People will say they don't have a proper job if they have time to read, and all the rest!"

This "and all the rest" was clearly the worst danger, a sign of these men's pride and their fear of books.

Francis was also scared of books, but he was convinced that they contained the world. The entire world. He wanted to bring that here, and if he'd been honest and thought for a little longer, he'd have realized that the person he most wanted to bring that world to was Marie-Jeanne. So he donned his kid gloves and carried on, otherwise by winter's end the interest payments for his mobile library would have brought him to his knees.

14

Too Loud a Silence

It might well have been Vida Lagetto who raised his spirits. Vida Lagetto—way up there at the world's end, on the cusp of the sky. Louis the Fourth started its promotional tour by toiling through the winding Trente Pas gorge, occasionally disappearing from sight behind a crag, before it turned right in Saint Ferréol onto a track signposted—more out of courtesy than anything else—as the D186 to Chaudon and finally drew up outside probably the region's best-hidden hotel, La Dolce Vita, which nestled below the summit of Mount Renard.

The mighty amphitheater of the Baronnies massif looked even more impressive from up here than it did from Condorcet. The lower slopes of the Bluye and the peak of Saint Julien fanned out in a palette of colors shading from green into gray and back again. Beyond them loomed the more intimate but savage face of Mont Ventoux and, above it, its white crown. If anywhere could be deemed the end of the world, the abandoned hamlet of La Dolce Vita was a good candidate.

It was the solitude and silence of the mountains that lured

the first few guests here. Most of them were drained from living in big, noisy cities and longed for something more picturesque, more dramatic, more sentimental. They ate well; slept for a long time; dreamed different, more intensive, more nonsensical, and more colorful dreams; and took aimless hikes in the mountains. After a few days in this peaceful no-man's-land, surrounded by the sounds of nature, they would dive back, dizzy with confusion, into the thundering maelstrom of their daily lives once more. The silence was hard to bear. Lovers withdrew from the outside world to La Dolce Vita—and so did people mending their broken hearts.

Beautiful and peaceful as the place was, even this small trickle of guests gradually dried up. Maybe it was simply too beautiful, too peaceful.

Francis knew Vida, the hotel's owner, because he would often make deliveries of sugar, lightbulbs, or a spare part for the generator that pumped water from the spring. The hotel had thirteen rooms, each with its own private terrace so that no guest was forced to speak to anyone else. Only at night might you hear the sobs of someone who had fallen out of love or the sighs of lovers united as one body.

Vida Lagetto's great, yearning heart

Vida Lagetto. There were wild horses in her heart; her birthplace, Villeperdrix, in her blood; and the salty freedom of the distant sea on her skin. She was haunted by so many dreams and thoughts about the world beyond the thyme-scented hills, and yet even as a child, she had gotten up every morning at half past four to help her father set tables and bake the day's bread. Only then would she go off to school, and going meant walking the many miles down to Condorcet and back. After supper she did her homework, always on the same table in the restaurant lounge—under a print of Antoine Serra's *Seated Nude Woman* at table 11, where otherwise only the mayor of Buis-les-Baronnies would sometimes sit with his favorite female assistant. Sooner or later, Vida would pay a visit to the kitchen, manned by its one-chef team, where there was always work for a patient young pair of hands. From the Corsican chef's loud exchanges with her Neapolitan father she learned what men valued in women and realized at an early age that she possessed none of those attributes. She was neither unapproachable nor foxy; she was no temptress and didn't think she could ever be forward. She was herself, that was all.

She finished school, and although her mind roamed far and wide, she stayed where she was, in her father's hotel, and gradually acquired his skills, from the cellar to the attic, from reception to calculations, from decorating to inventories, from repairing the generator to mending the rounded roof tiles known locally as "nuns and monks." She consoled herself with the idea that the world came to her and not the other way around.

Vida watched people. She learned to read people's beds, their faces in the candlelight, the words they whispered to each other under the spell of a rare champagne or one of the copper-colored wines from the vineyards clustered around Mont Ventoux. She watched how restless the deep surrounding silence made them as the sounds they couldn't otherwise hear grew louder inside them.

Sometimes she would stand in front of the mirror at

night, especially when the full moon was so bright that her body cast a shadow. She would examine her nakedness and think how wasted it was, that she was withering away without ever having flowered. As she caressed her curves and soft contours, a shiver ran through her, chilling her to the bone, at the knowledge that this body recalled no other and no one remembered her skin either. One day, she thought, it would be as if she had never existed.

Vida too raged against me in her own quiet way. She wasn't bitter, merely sad, and her sadness was full of resignation. She was no longer waiting. She was no longer looking.

What she didn't know was that she had already been found.

She didn't know this and so she loved everyone equally, to the best of her ability. She took care of those who came to her, offering them sleep, food, and soft light: This was her way of showing her love and a substitute for wrapping herself around any one man.

Vida Lagetto was a rare treasure in a noisy and often distrustful age. She had a gift for enveloping other people with a respect that was blind to their characteristics, their flaws, their misdeeds and lies. This had always been the case since the days when she observed how her father was a father to each and every guest. Not just a father, no; a great papa-mama-being, father and mother rolled into one, strict and nurturing, protective and imperious. And sometimes more of a mama and papa to his guests than to his own daughter.

Even he couldn't prevent the guests from growing uneasy at the great peace and quiet, though. It wasn't enough to build them a swimming pool or stock the cellar with fine wines. It wasn't enough that they were surrounded by dozens of types of birds they had never seen before, such as owls screeching in the night; butterflies and foxes flitting through the grounds; lavender bushes and benches under the olive tree.

What on earth could she do to enable them to put up with themselves here amid all this beauty that demonstrated how remote most people are from life's beauties most of the time?

If this continued, they would soon have only one guest, a regular called Édouard, who was more silent than the mountains; she really didn't get what he saw in this place. And when that happened, she would have to close down her little world and leave it behind.

What then?

Vida was scared. She had never tried leaving this nest clinging to the mountainside.

Then, one day, Francis Meurienne and Marie-Jeanne came spluttering up the hillside in the 2CV. He lifted the canisters of olive oil Vida had ordered out of the back of his van and described his freshly devised plans for a mobile library.

The future mobile librarian had concocted a little speech for Vida Lagetto and was now hoping he wouldn't sound uneducated or stammer like an idiot.

"Books are like landscapes," he began. "A landscape doesn't teach us anything, but through gazing at it we discover ourselves and—"

"Stop right there!" she said.

"I'm sorry?"

Vida shut her eyes. She pinched the top of her nose between thumb and forefinger and shook her head. "How could I . . . ?" she mumbled.

Francis feared the worst.

"You don't need to sell me books like melons from Carpentras."

"I don't?"

"No. You just need to explain one thing to me."

"Um, yes?" Francis said warily.

"Why has this idea only just struck you now, *mon cher* monsieur?" She beamed at him, and that beaming smile was like sunrise, sunset, and everything in between.

"Well, the idea only just came to me. My mistake, *ma chère* madame."

"This changes everything, you see," Vida said, her voice quivering with excitement. "I think you may just have saved my hotel. I think you might save all of us. I think—"

"I don't think so. Most fathers are, um, well, a bit reluctant when it comes to books."

"Why are you talking to the men about books?"

"Oh," Francis said, and after a few more seconds, "I see."

He looked at Marie-Jeanne, who was staring at Vida with her head cocked.

"Talk to the women, Monsieur Meurienne. Women are less scared of change."

Vida was experiencing an avalanche of insights. Wow! Why hadn't *she* come up with this idea for healing the inexplicable suffering of her guests?

That was it! Books! She'd done exactly that as a young girl, dreaming the nights away in other places. She had been hurt by Rochester with Jane Eyre, and last year she had read

One Hundred Years of Solitude and been glad that she was alive today.

Books. People could use them to hide away from the voices inside their heads. What was it that Francis had blurted out? "Like landscapes." Yes, books were places. Places of refuge. Places of peace.

And that was how Vida selected her first dozen books, including *Jane Eyre, Great Expectations,* and *Metamorphoses*. She invited Francis onto the terrace, served him a strong coffee with a little hot milk, and half an hour later she handed him a list of questions to give to the bookseller in Nyons for his careful yet puzzled consideration.

She was looking for:

+ books for people with broken hearts
+ books for people who have walked out on their families
+ books for people who wonder if they are living the right life
+ books to read before saying farewell
+ books for people who have too many possessions and still want more
+ and, please, books for people who lose their tongues precisely when they should open their hearts

Francis studied the list, decrypting the name of each category in Vida's eccentric handwriting, and asked, "You think the bookseller knows all these things?"

"If he's as good a bookseller as I've heard, he'll know what I mean," Vida said decisively. "And if not, he can go to hell."

Francis thought that he would like to be able to talk about books the way Madame Lagetto did. How many would he have to read, though? A thousand? And how long would he need? A hundred years or so?

"Come along," she said to Marie-Jeanne. "Let's look for a good place for La Dolce Vita's new library."

Marie-Jeanne followed Vida, her eyes firmly trained on the woman's twinkle. The lights were in the lovely soft spot between Vida's shoulders and the back of her neck, and her glow was very faint. It no longer had enough energy to shine brightly.

15

Wanted: Someone with Extensive Local Knowledge

From that moment on, Francis would always ask to talk to the lady of the house first when he made his rounds. Next, he would lend a hand to the men as they tilled or tended their fields, whispering into their ear at an opportune moment.

"You know, Laurent, they're not going to respect you if you're scared of books. And borrowing a book is a whole lot cheaper than buying a radio set."

He said the same to Maurice and Bobo.

"Really? How much is it?"

The loan fee was fifty centimes per book, slightly less than the price of a baguette. Also, if someone borrowed ten books, the eleventh was free. Francis told the men that their wives had borrowed some already and were in a very good mood.

"In a good mood? Really? Why didn't you say so from the start?"

Third, he would take along a Marcel Pagnol book for the cantankerous old men, for where was the "water of the hills" not a scarce resource? What's more, Pagnol was one of their own.

His fourth method was something Marie-Jeanne had suggested after giving the matter considerable thought. She would talk to the children.

"And why do you think that will encourage their parents to sign up?"

"Well, Petitpa, because we ruffle your feathers."

"Feathers? What feathers?"

But she was already bounding off to see the little children and the not-so-little ones. She told them about the barefoot writer (Françoise Sagan), magical romances, and secret Hobbit holes in invisible realms (J. R. R. Tolkien). She told them that girls were allowed to wear trousers (Enid Blyton's *The Famous Five*) and that books could teach you how to speak to ghosts and breed worms as well as the truth about Christmas (Charles Darwin). The result was that some parental feathers were seriously ruffled.

Suddenly, things were moving.

Marie-Jeanne stared the men down—these fierce badgers and fearful mountain bears. Francis watched their proud, anxious gazes gradually become soft and translucent. The girl would look them in the eye and nod—just a hint of a nod—and within a minute the old folks seemed to breathe more easily.

They grumbled, "Oh all right then, we'll give it a go."

Sometimes she would casually add a slightly strange remark, such as: "Your wife has delightful elbows" or "Do you comb your wife's hair sometimes?" When Francis asked her what a particular comment was supposed to mean, she would simply shake her head and say, "That's a top-secret secret."

Some of these top-secret secrets

+ The parts of every person that Marie-Jeanne could now see shining: their mouths, hands, shoulders, elbows, and cheeks, the backs of their necks, and, in rare cases, their earlobes, the tips of their noses, a knee, or one specific toe.

+ Since Loulou and Luca had started ignoring each other, their lights had gotten hiccups and looked off-color.

+ Marie-Jeanne read comics on the toilet like the cheese-making farmer, Maurice.

+ She regarded books as like the sea—she could swim through them. When she had finished her first one, she had simply reached out for the closest one to hand. She had carried on doing so every evening and had started getting up earlier and earlier each morning too. Her plan was to look back at the end of her life over the long and exciting course she had swum through times and hearts and currents of knowledge and different worlds and emotions—and it should make it easier for her to accept death. Meanwhile, just in case, she jotted down the names of all the authors she wanted to meet on the other side. The list was already very long. Would one deathtime be enough to meet them all and ask them what it was like to be a writer?

+ None of the books she had read said anything about the strange illuminations around people's bodies.

+ Sometimes when she looked up from her book she got the feeling she had learned a great deal about people. But then her mind would turn to Luca and Loulou and all the others, and it seemed as if she were peering out through a tiny book-shaped window of knowledge into a vast, fog-shrouded landscape. There was so much she didn't know.

+ She continued to ponder the immense sadness Madame Châtelet kept bottled up deep inside herself, like a wounded animal in a dark forest. She thought about Madame Colette too. And Vida Lagetto. All of them were missing something. Marie-Jeanne ached in a place where she didn't usually feel pain. In her heart. She made scrupulously sure that she kept this secret because she could not figure out why it hurt.

Fifth, Francis visited all the local councillors again. They appeared from behind their bakery counters and cheese displays and anvils with a show of irritation, sighing at the prospect of what this weirdo in his strange van might want this time.

"May I ask you another question?" Francis generally began.

"Go ahead."

"What annoys you most about young people today?"

"Ha! I can tell you that without thinking. They start something and then don't stick it out. Around here, though, you have to stick it out to the end."

Francis would place one of Thomas Mann's novels or *Robinson Crusoe* in front of them.

"This," he said, "has a lot of long sentences. So long that you sometimes wonder how many years might have gone by while you've been reading it and if you're ever going to escape from it alive."

"So?"

"So, it's only by starting and seeing if you can stick it out that you see if you have the mettle or not." He would pick up the book again from the flour-covered counter or a table smeared with dubbin. "But my guess is you wouldn't make it. None of you men would. Nor any of your sons either. You said so yourself—they wouldn't stick it out." Francis slapped his hand down proprietorially on the book cover.

The man's eyes narrowed. "Oh, you don't think so?"

"Nope, I don't. Want to bet on it?"

"Okay, deal."

"Oh, and while we're on the subject, *The Catcher in the Rye* will tell you exactly what your boys get up to in the hay barn. They won't even need to come clean to you. You can read it all here."

Salinger's book came thudding down on top of the cheese display case. This time Francis had wheedled some information out of Colette about the lesson you got from such a "textbook for life."

"Take this too. *To Kill a Mockingbird* will tell you a thing or two about how to deal with people who still look down on your Italian ancestry." *Bang*—Harper Lee's novel had landed.

Defoe and Salinger and Lee stayed in the village for several weeks and were returned bent and bruised, accompanied by a curt inquiry about when Francis planned to visit next. The men said that there was a contest to see who could read the fattest doorstopper and cotton on fastest to what he could learn from a page-turner. Damn kids—the worst thing about them was that they didn't believe that oldies had once been young themselves. Now, though, the councillors would show them what staying power meant. They wouldn't be taken for fools again.

"Give me your thickest book."

"Okay then, how about *War and Peace*? Two thousand two hundred twenty-eight pages."

"Great title. What's it about?"

"Exactly what it says on the cover."

"Hand it over."

"You'll never finish it."

"Want to bet, Francis?"

"Hmm, better not. You're a man of unsuspected abilities."

There was a triumphant smile on the man's face and a quiet grin on Francis's as five ten-centime coins changed hands.

Sixth, Francis put out an advert that read as follows: *Wanted: person with driver's license, local knowledge, and flexible schedule for mobile library.*

He received only one application.

No, it wasn't from the part-time solicitor Géraldine Châtelet. Although she could drive and possessed an abundance of the other two qualities, why should she suddenly change her lifestyle so radically?

Incidentally, Géraldine had sat there for hours after that famous night, chastising herself. She had looked at herself in the mirror out of the two girls' line of sight, and she hadn't liked the woman she saw staring back.

I've become a coward, she thought, *who gets up in the morning, turns on the heater, puts on the kettle, makes her bed, and checks twice that there isn't a speck of dust where it shouldn't be. A woman who arranges her hair carefully before going out in public and never steps out into the street without changing her underwear.* (Because how embarrassing if she were to have an accident outside the Bar du Centre, run over by a car or struck down by a falling airplane part. She'd have to lie there in the ambulance in her dirty underwear!) *A cowardly woman who saves face, goes along with the whole charade, keeps her chin up, and so forth, waging a war of attrition against herself. Someone who is only brave enough to live in her imagination.*

Mechanically, she picked up a book. It was Jean-Paul Sartre's play *No Exit,* and her finger came to rest on the oft-quoted and generally interpreted line: "Hell is other people."

She swept the book off the table with her arm.

"Betraying yourself—that's the real hell."

How, Géraldine asked herself, *did that sense of having the world at my feet magically vanish?*

Paralyzed, she had seen the joy she had once tasted walk away and hoped she might erase all memory of it. Delete it so she could live a tame, joyless life. Immerse herself in her work to be sure she'd forget it. Plunge into the world of tango so that, for the space of three *canzoni* or a *tanda,* she might find some peace in the arms of a stranger without—ever!—getting too close to a man. *Anything but another fall from grace,* she thought. She wouldn't survive a second time.

And now? Now she thought she'd been a coward. A coward in love.

And no, she couldn't change that overnight.

How to change your life

There are serious suggestions that from the first timid stirrings of an urge for existential change ("Should I change my life or just veg out?") to the start of a new life ("Yes! And what's more, right away!"), it generally takes seven years.

But . . . those seven years had now passed for another person, in the following manner.

16

To the Barricades!

For seven years before the fateful day she got into her red 2CV to talk to Francis about the second mobile librarian post, sixty-three-year-old Valérie Montesquieu had lived alone in her house tucked away in a remote corner of the modern world.

Her garden on the slopes above the river Lance was a wondrous wilderness, and Valérie had dropped off the world's radar. She didn't need light at night. Not once. Not for a long time. She had been padding around her house in the dark for seven years and knew every sharp edge, every door handle, every floorboard.

She walked and lived without a sound. Even her breathing was colorless. She didn't speak because inside her head she couldn't stop talking to the voice that had left her. She replayed every word of over forty years of conversations.

Valérie left the garden to its own devices. She imagined the garden was female; she gave her the freedom to destroy and reshape herself as she saw fit, creating tangled grottoes of light and oleander bushes in which to lose herself. The garden brought the summer back from the dead, and there were scattered butterflies and sandy hollows where the sparrows bathed on hot days. In the winter she tasted the wind, and every spring she once again forgot who she had been.

They got on well, Valérie and the garden.

There was a similar pattern to her library. It was arranged like a moth's flightpath. Coincidental, darting and flitting this way and that, sometimes dazzled by colors and shapes, sobered by the contents, always hungry. Her library was like her garden. It resisted any constraint and all around, trees of books rose up out of the shadows and climbed the curtains and the sides of the chairs.

Valérie didn't want to see herself, not without the person she used to live with. She couldn't have coped.

The shadows of that person were allowed to linger in dark corners, but not in the light.

She had lived alone with books for even longer. As a girl she had stolen hundreds of matches from her father's desk and hidden them in a cigarillo box she had secretly salvaged from his wastepaper bin. From the inside of the box came a scent of vanilla, and the outside smelled of him—his hands, his aftershave lotion, and the saddle leather he had touched and treated all day. It gave off his warmth, a fragrance she had draped around herself as an oversoul she could snuggle up inside.

Valérie had never pinched a whole box, only ever two to five matches at a time. She always carried a few loose ones around in her pockets, and she never told her mother why she didn't want a skirt like all the other girls but trousers, which she hid under her school skirt. She knew her mother wouldn't understand; she was less sure of her father's views on the matter.

She placed the matches between the pages of her books.

She did this so that the pages wouldn't crumble and so the binding didn't press them together too tightly, trapping and freezing the characters forever in this enchanted castle of words and suspended time. To ensure they didn't have to endure the same story on repeat, the same death, the same loves. The same day, over and over again. There had to be a tiny opening through which the characters could escape if they so wished.

When Valérie grew up, she ran a bookshop in the small town of Gap and met people who came to represent her world. Then, seven years ago, the love of her life died. There was one night when she decided to erase herself with a letter opener. She sat at the tiny bureau in the darkest corner of her living room, sharpening the blade. But nothing came of it, which probably doesn't come as a surprise by this point.

Amazing as it sounds, someone broke into her house that same night. A young man. He entered through a window, having obviously misinterpreted the silence and darkness of the house with the wild garden. He was only a novice, and when he had picked himself up from the floor after tripping over mountains of books and an armchair, they settled down for a chat.

"I'm sorry," Valérie said, "but I wasn't expecting any visitors. Oh, by the way, you're sitting on *Madame Bovary*."

His face was in shadow, and so was hers. The moonlight lit up only the windowsill and a patch of floorboards, her hands and his, his knee in a pair of work trousers and hers in some culottes whose pockets were stuffed with matches.

"What do you mean? Madame who?" the young man's lovely voice said from the darkness.

"Emma Bovary. She is married and neglected, has an affair, finds it just as bad, and kills herself. A French classic whose purpose is to teach women to be modest. You're sitting on it."

"Oh," he said, "I'm sorry." But having removed the copy of Flaubert's novel from under his backside, he didn't know where to put it.

"If you've never heard of it, take it with you."

"Um, I don't read very much."

"So what *do* you do to find out more about yourself? Break into women's houses?"

At first there was no answer, then he said faintly, "Are you going to call the gendarmes?"

"Would you like that?"

"I wouldn't, if possible. I'd rather read *Madame Bovary*."

"Yes, I should think that's possible," Valérie said. "In fact, I would rather you started reading it straightaway too. It helps—with everything."

"Everything? Really?"

Bon sang, Valérie thought, *burglars aren't what they used to be. Then again, is anyone what they used to be?*

They carried on talking, cautiously, warily, throughout the night. All night long. The not-so-young woman and the still-young man, whose name might have been Antoine or Georges or Tiago—she didn't ask.

He mentioned a girl who didn't even notice that he was alive, and Valérie suggested he give her a book, but not necessarily *Madame Bovary*. She talked about how she now believed that death was female, and he said that life might be like a book: If you took your own life, you'd never know how it ended.

At dawn the two survivors parted. They had both resolved to be less cowardly, and that day Valérie went out and bought a newspaper for the first time in years to find out which damn year it was. She had read Francis's advert, replied to it, and now here she was.

After getting out of her car, Valérie put up an elegant, white, lace-edged parasol and walked no less elegantly toward the house.

Francis showed her onto the small stone terrace, which was protected from the sun by a sail-shaped raffia awning. She requested a glass of cold water with a drop of raspberry syrup in it. Marie-Jeanne asked if she might sit in on their conversation.

Valérie had that kind of aura: Her appearance put everyone around her on their best behavior.

"May I ask why you are interested in this not-exactly-unexacting job, Madame Montesquieu?"

She studied Francis, and everything about her was so delicate and dainty, like a china doll with lots of beautiful wrinkles.

"Freedom," she said simply.

"Yes, well," Francis replied, "the freedom is, um, relative. The working hours are governed by the market days—"

Valérie interrupted him by raising her rolled-up tiny parasol.

"Freedom, my dear boy"—this was clearly what Francis was from her perspective—"freedom of the spirit is the only thing worth achieving every day, even in limited freedom from time pressure. For that is what we shall do here—we shall achieve freedom."

"Ah yes, my thoughts entirely . . . if I'd spent a very long time thinking about it," Francis said.

"Because freedom," Valérie continued, "begins where

you first overstep your boundaries. And where is that?" Here she jabbed the tip of her parasol at Marie-Jeanne.

The girl thought about it before answering, "Um, I'm not very good at geography."

"It's all in your mind. Only in your mind! The boundaries of knowledge, education, and socially constructed conventions. Of fear, self-imposed rules, and so on and so forth. And nothing—I repeat, nothing—is a more discreet and incorruptible accomplice than literature." Valérie stood up as she proclaimed these words, but her head remained at the same height as when she was sitting down.

She had made herself clear, though. For Madame Valérie Pénélope Montesquieu, the mobile library was the next French Revolution, and she was determined to wield her lace-trimmed parasol on the foremost barricades.

She smiled, and it looked as if her face were astonished to remember how it felt to be happy.

"Also, I urgently need to find an occupation to stop myself from going completely gaga, quite apart from the fact that my savings have dwindled like a bar of soap."

"In that case," Francis said, "you're hired."

Marie-Jeanne refereed a game of rock paper scissors to decide their routes. Valérie set out for the Drôme in Louis the Fourth, while Francis took Louis the Fifth on the Vaucluse run, and Louis the Third enjoyed a well-earned rest.

They debated which books they should stock up on, and Francis repeated the guidelines that Vida had given him.

" 'Books for people with broken hearts. Books for people who have walked out on their families. Books for people who are wondering if they're in the right life. Books to read before saying farewell. Books for people who have too many possessions but still want more. And please, some books for people who lose their tongues precisely when they should open their hearts.' "

Smiling, Valérie added, "We also need books for children, books for children who want to stop being children, books for women, books for men, and books for people who don't care if they are a child, a woman, a man, or a seahorse. . . . And I pray to Thoth and Hermes Trismegistus, the gods of writing, that this last category will grow and grow."

"Seahorses?"

"Those who don't care what sex someone is and just treat everyone alike."

So now they could get started. And the winner was whoever could say "Trismegistus" quickest.

17

Francis Meets the Rolling Stones. Sort Of.

News of the mobile library got around. Children talked about the delivery service at school and at home, and so their mothers and aunts and grandmothers came to hear about the system of literary loans and orders. They saw the rattling 2CVs as a new and unhoped-for source of happiness, bringing books that cost virtually nothing directly to their doors. And adding something unusual and precious to their lives—time to themselves.

Cautiously, these mothers and daughters, aunts and grandmothers, tried on this new opportunity for size. They'd never realized how well it would suit them and how much good it would do them to have time to themselves.

Hitherto they had spent every waking hour making themselves useful. But no one had really paid much attention to this because it consisted of tidying up, mending clothes, cooking, washing, and keeping quiet. All the things the world thought a good person—and especially a good woman—ought to do.

Suddenly they could recognize themselves in a book. Reinvent themselves. Not be useful, not always beautiful. They blossomed, they had new thoughts, they developed a greater sensitivity, and suddenly their inner worlds stretched and expanded and they could breathe more easily.

The first commune had taken root in the valley of Les Pilles, only a few miles from Nyons. While the established local families were still trying to come to terms with the fact that it wasn't the fifties anymore, the commune dwellers were so far ahead of their time that they might have arrived from the future.

Francis was full of tense anticipation as he drove toward the commune, which had coalesced around a Parisian professor and had an *épicerie* that Marie-Jeanne thought always reeked of burnt thyme (we'll leave her to enjoy that illusion until sooner or later someone tells her that the aroma of smoldering hashish smells a bit like the wild herbs of Provence).

He didn't really understand the words these people used. Words like "flower power," "hippies," and "existentialism."

They were academics, intellectuals, musicians, and other people who had dropped out of mainstream society in order to come up with new rules for themselves and for life, and to grow and sell fruit and vegetables. Would they laugh at him? Or he at them? He considered that there was no need for coaxing turnips out of the unwilling soil to become a religion.

The dropout professor from Paris, his long hair floating over unshaven cheeks and a buttoned-up white linen shirt, surprised shy Francis by giving him a hug and two air kisses on each side instead of the usual one. He offered Francis a cup of herbal tea (Francis sipped it warily in case he started to feel high as a kite) and then took a close look at Francis's higgledy-piggledy collection of literature.

"You are a secret revolutionary, *mon cher* Meurienne," the Parisian professor said.

"You're too kind, monsieur."

"Kind? Not at all—it's merely the truth. Your concept of the common good, combined with an individualism that looks beyond its own boundaries, which will in turn change the community—that is modern revolution. Without bloodshed and yet with total determination."

"Oh. Right." Maybe Francis should drink some more of this funny tea to keep up with this man's reasoning.

"Aha!" the professor suddenly exclaimed, holding up a new acquisition that Meurienne's team had discussed long and hard with Mussigmann the bookseller because it was a difficult read. *As I Lay Dying* by William Faulkner. Half the population of a village tells stories of heat waves and fire and other disasters during a long march, stories of bleak farming lives, secrets revealed, who went with whom and why and whose children. . . . Not a romantic idyll, by any stretch.

("Exactly!" Valérie had said. "Literature is not a cakewalk. We all need a good shake of scouring powder on our souls from time to time.")

The Parisian's eyes were moist as he said, "I read this when I was a young man, and ever since I have felt a longing. A longing to be here, right here"—he gestured at his surroundings—"immersed in real life. But I lost the book—you could say I lost my common sense after swapping it for the idiocy of convention, which produces only artificial life." He stood up and embraced Francis again. The bookman had no idea what was going on and no idea what to do with his arms, so he opted to give the agitated man a fatherly pat on the back and mumbled, "Don't worry, you'll be fine."

He realized that people might read the same book, but to each of them it was different. Valérie had described it as scouring powder, but to this man it was . . . What was it exactly? A long-lost friend. It was amazing.

"You must come every week," the professor ordered. "Books remind us of who we once wanted to be."

The librarian gave a quiet cough. Dear God, he had no trouble recalling what he used to want to do—he wanted to repair things—but, hey . . .

Francis received his first order from another commune dweller and added it scrupulously to Vida's wish list. A Swedish booklet with strange, um, hydraulic contortions.

He sat there for a little longer, listening to the commune's residents discussing liberation and guilt complexes and homeopathy. Perhaps this was a new age? In any case, they had good taste in music, and for a second Francis was tempted by the idea of starting up a mobile music library.

But music caused even more conflict between the generations than books, which were noiseless until you opened them. The Rolling Stones, though. They were pretty heavy. Hey, hey, hey.

Elsa Malbec kept a record of the loans. She always knew who had which book. This gave her a window into the secrets of the community as well as earning her new respect because she never disclosed who had borrowed the Angélique novels yet again—the leathery skin on that nasty cobbler's fingers was softening as he eschewed his pincers and shoemaker's thread to leaf delicately through a book—or had returned them in a deplorable condition.

"It's called literary privacy," Elsa declared with the kind of pride doctors, lawyers, and confessors take in their oaths of confidentiality.

It was amazing, what people got up to with books. Francis and Marie-Jeanne found traces of sheep dung, coffee grounds, and crumbs of pipe tobacco between the pages, and one time even a live shiny green beetle. The beetle had somehow ended up in a book by Sartre, and this intrigued Francis so much that he laboriously read a few lines for the first time.

The sentence the beetle had been hiding was this: "Life has no meaning a priori. Before you come alive, life is nothing. It is up to you to give it a meaning, and that value is nothing but the meaning that you choose."

"All right," Francis said, "but what does 'a priori' mean?"

" 'In advance,' " replied Marie-Jeanne, who every day read the book at the top of the pile of new acquisitions, whether it was by Jules Verne, Friedrich Nietzsche, T. S. Eliot, or Jane Austen. " 'In principle.' "

"So why didn't he write that?"

"He wants to show that he's read Kant."

"Um, who's he again?"

"He was the guy who said we should all use our own reason."

"Who else's would we use?"

Reading the sentence again, Francis found it a bit long. Then he thought about it and pondered what he hadn't known about Kant a priori but now did. He decided that even though he'd known it all along, he still liked how it sounded.

Books at least made you think things over, he thought,

just as Madame Brillant had predicted. It was different from ordinary thinking. Ordinary thinking revolved around questions such as what he was going to eat, how he'd get the money to pay for the food, looking after the car's spark plugs, and that kind of thing. Book thinking was, um, flightier. It turned ordinary thoughts into buzzards. Maybe he should give books another go. Just not one by this weird bloke with his glasses and "a priori"s.

Naturally, Marie-Jeanne kept all the things she found inside books in another chest.

Torn-off tickets for the cinema in Cavaillon.

A shopping list: "Chestnuts. Matches. Magnifying glass."

A postcard from Venice.

Once, she even found the first lines of a letter: "I send this thought to you on a night when the stars are falling from the sky. I don't know your face. I don't know your name, and I won't tell you mine. The day we stand face-to-face, the day we touch, we will know we are the ones." It had been inserted into *Gravity and Grace* by Simone Weil.

Simone Weil . . . The philosopher, she thought. *Géraldine Châtelet's favorite author. Who was she writing to? Why is love so tentative? Why does it hurt both when it's not there and when it's there?*

"Petitpa?"

"Hmm?"

"Why is love so hard?"

"Well . . ." Francis pulled up a three-legged stool. "You know, it's . . ." He sighed and tried again. "Love is. That's really the only thing we know for sure."

"What is it?"

"Just that: *It is*. That we can say for sure. Love *is*. It exists. It is here. That much is certain. We don't know anything more about it and we cannot describe it. Do you see what I mean?"

"Er, I don't think I do actually," Marie-Jeanne said.

I quietly sat down next to them.

Francis took a deep breath. Why couldn't she ask him something less important? If he said the wrong thing, she would carry his nonsense out into the world with her, and who knows, his words might wreck every date, hope, and desire she ever had. He didn't want that. He wanted her to contemplate her future life like it was a river of wonder and possibilities.

He screwed up all his courage, for what was the point of being a father if he couldn't do his best to explain love to his daughter?

"Love *is*. We agree on that, right? It *is*. Like the sea, like the sun, like the mountains. That tells us nothing about . . . how long it will last. Or what color it is. Or what form it will take. Like the sea, the sun, and the mountains, it is always different."

"In fairy tales, lovers always live happily ever after. But that's just a diplomatic lie, isn't it?"

Francis rubbed his hands together in his discomfort. He didn't want to disappoint his child. He wanted her to trust her gut feeling. The way he trusted his gut feeling, which told him, for example, that Elsa's affection was really taking a very, um, extraordinarily unusual form.

She loved him as she could, not as he might want. And if you could come to terms with the idea that you'd never be loved the way you wanted and only the way the other person was capable of loving you right then, you could rest easy.

Sometimes it is the kindest, most altruistic people who are the most intelligent, not people in universities. The sort of person who sits on a stool in a messy barn, attempting to tackle his eleven-year-old's queries about love.

"Sometimes love *is* like in a fairy tale," Francis tried again, "but sometimes love is completely different. Fleeting, like a fragrance you'll never forget, even though you've smelled it only once. Maybe that fragrance only existed for that one afternoon. Maybe a walk when everything was completely calm, clear, and heartbreaking. He loves her and she loves him. But before the two of them become each other's brightest star, each other's greatest stroke of luck, she tells him, 'You'll suffer too much. You mustn't stop loving your children and your wife, and so I'm letting you go. As much as I love you, however much I know you love me. Now go, go quickly.' "

"She loves him so much she lets him go so he won't be unhappy?"

"That's right. He'll obviously be upset because he's losing her, but less unhappy than if he lost his existing life. And they have loved each other—or will all their lives, even if they never speak to each other again. That's happiness."

"No, it isn't—it's horrible. Why do we even have to go through such happiness?"

"Maybe we have the wrong idea about happiness. Happiness doesn't mean always being happy or that everything's easy. And yet we still have happiness. Because we love even when it hurts. It is everything. And when I say everything, I mean *everything*."

"Hmm," Marie-Jeanne said.

Francis dug awkwardly through a pile of old gramophone horns, wind chimes, and broken nutcrackers. How could he illustrate to his foster daughter that not everything you experienced in love was useful and sometimes it certainly wasn't nice?

Aha! His hand alighted on a tiny sofa from a dollhouse.

"Love is a house, Marie-Jeanne. Everything in a house is supposed to be used, not kept under wraps or 'protected.' Only those who live in all areas of love, avoiding none of its rooms or doors, are fully alive. Arguing and caressing are equally important, as are embracing and pushing each other away. Every single room of the house of love needs to be inhabited, or else ghosts and gossip will settle in and make themselves at home. Neglected rooms can turn spiteful and start to stink."

He rummaged around in Marie-Jeanne's chest and built a small dollhouse from all the curiosities collected there. The girl helped him, leaving all the miniature doors open, and the dollhouse was inhabited by all the forgotten things that someone had once loved.

After a while she pulled out the most recent pile of returned books. "What should I do about these, Petitpa?"

"About what?"

"These. Look." Almost every book bore the tracks of a sob or traces of a borrower's sadness. It was shocking to realize that books could transform glowing into weeping.

Francis picked up a book and inspected it from every angle. "This one looks fine." He couldn't see what Marie-Jeanne saw.

They wiped and cleaned and stacked the books and repaired minor tears.

After a while, the girl asked, "Will someone love me when I grow up?"

Francis looked at the girl he cherished as if she were his natural daughter. Her otherwise bright and lively eyes had taken on the color of despair, something he had never observed in her gaze before.

"Of course someone will. Your prince has already been born. He's already out there looking for you."

I stayed there by their side. The most natural course of events would have been to lift my hand and put a sign on Marie-Jeanne. I'd already decided where it would be. In her eyes. My dearest wish was that she should be seen for what she was one day. She would recognize the person for whom she was a river of wonder by the fact that he would look her straight in the eye and understand her immediately and absolutely. I would select him with the utmost care. She should be loved and she should feel free and safe. I wanted to make Francis's promise to her come true.

But as I raised my fingers to put a mark on Marie-Jeanne, I couldn't do it. It wasn't possible. I couldn't touch her.

18

Bonjour, the Bookabus Is Here

The mobile library soon came to be known as the "book bus," and because children couldn't separate the two words, they called it the "bookabus" and the name stuck.

Valérie Montesquieu and Francis Meurienne drove their books anywhere there was a road or a track, and when the tracks ended, Marie-Jeanne mounted Fino the donkey to bring "knowledge, education, and beauty, not to mention some of the most romantic stories on earth, to the all-too-austere wastelands," as Valérie put it.

Françoise Sagan, Anne Golon's series of Angélique novels, Jules Verne, and good old Simenon were popular, as were what Mussigmann the bookseller called "*romans à l'eau de rose*"—romances in which pirates, revolutionaries, and dukes fell madly in love with unhappily married damsels and absconded with them.

Simone de Beauvoir and *The Catcher in the Rye* enjoyed less enthusiastic uptake, and Francis and Valérie could only loan them after swearing absolute secrecy—cast-iron literary privacy. Sartre and Camus, Foucault and Simone Weil, were tricky propositions too. While the younger generation couldn't get enough of them, their elders were bamboozled as they read these books on their outdoor toilets; they had the feeling that these people were writing about them but not really for them. Only Madame Châtelet devoured the writings of the existentialists and women philosophers.

Loulou now reserved the finest baguettes for this elegant lady's secret dinners with her invisible guest. However, it was months before Madame Châtelet could look Loulou in the eye and say, "*Merci, ma belle,*" with a grateful nod.

Much to Elsa's satisfaction, the mobile library's biggest hit was her handwritten recipes. She dictated them to Marie-Jeanne, and there was huge demand for *Madame Elsa's Traditional Drôme Provençale Cookery Book*. Francis considered having it printed at the works below the castle in Grignan, but he calculated that even his rising earnings were insufficient to cover the costs.

So Marie-Jeanne transcribed ten copies in her best handwriting under the calligraphic guidance of Madame Colette. They bound them and Elsa made a lace cover for each, but ten was far too few—there was a months-long waiting list for them. Everyone wanted to know how to make her olive and truffle omelet, her scented scrambled eggs, her ratatouille seasoned with garlic and onions alone, no herbs. The book contained a magic formula for thyme brandy and recipes for homemade nougat, the region's famous *pô bouilli* rye bread, *gratin dauphinois, ravioles,* and garlic mayonnaise containing *alicoque,* new freshly pressed olive oil from Nyons.

Teachers, farmers, members of the Confrérie des Chevaliers de l'Olivier (an olive growers' guild whose honorary president was the author Jean Giono), the Society for the Preservation of Pétanque, young women who managed holiday camps in the Vaucluse region, Raspail the baker's five daughters, and everyone else was allowed to place an order to buy or borrow a particular book. Tactfully put, this resulted in an amazingly varied selection of tastefully printed French works, ranging from love stories to the most detailed guides to building a house or maintaining a chicken coop.

Nevertheless, Elsa, Valérie, and Marie-Jeanne were in charge of choosing the library's lending literature. Their advisers in this regard were the printer in Grignan, who got wind of new publications six months in advance; Monsieur Mussigmann the bookseller; and Madame Brillant, who had an infallible knack for predicting which books girls would love and their fathers would hate. They were joined on their informal committee by the author Jean Finkielkraut, who had moved back from Paris after the civil unrest of 1968 and was now living on a hill near Châteauneuf-de-Bordette in a region where, much to his disgust, no one had ever heard of him.

Jean Finkielkraut's glow was on his forehead. To Marie-Jeanne this made him look like a unicorn with a goatee.

"Oh, books!" the author exclaimed the first time Francis slogged his way up the winding path to the writer's tiny village. This was shortly after the librarian had attempted to explain what love was to Marie-Jeanne and built a dollhouse. "Books are life's most marvelous, its most essential, illusion. They give you more energy than the church and—"

"Sure," Francis said, "but no more than a good aioli does."

"What was the last thing you read?" Finkielkraut asked. He slyly hoped, despite his general decency, that the mobile librarian would say his betting slips so the author might look down on him with a blend of mild irony and paternalistic condescension for the rest of their days.

"Sartre," Francis said truthfully.

"Oh."

"He was a big fan of Kant," Francis added. "Not a priori, but over time."

Well, I'll be damned, thought Finkielkraut with the exhilarating feeling that he'd found a soulmate here in the back of beyond.

Friendship

Friends are the people who stick around through thick and thin to suggest, "To hell with it—let's go for a drink." That, in any case, is what Jean Finkielkraut had had in mind when he was looking for friends in Paris and found none. Friendship there was a matter of shared political values, and he'd grown sick of it.

With Francis, Jean experienced friendship as a relationship based on very little talking (on Francis's part) and much more doing. This led to his delightful realization that his body was intended for more than simply to carry his head around.

He learned to pick Nyons's black Tanche olives (by hand—the olive trees were never combed in Nyons because this damaged the delicate branches) and never to eat them straight from the tree (they had to be soaked in water first and then preserved in brine before they would reveal their secrets). Francis also taught him that all donkeys are a little deafer in one ear. He learned to imitate the call of the little owl and stand like a real Nyons man at the counter of Luc le Marseillais's Bar du Centre (keep your arms crossed and resting on the bar and, whatever happens, only abandon this stoic position to take a swig). His friend also demonstrated how to hold nails between your lips during DIY so you didn't hurt yourself. In general, the man from Paris did all the things he'd always been itching to do. He carved wooden figures, he prepared and cooked an unfortunate rabbit (in white wine), and he could soon wedge his knee under the steering wheel to allow him, for example, to roll a cigarette and drive at the same time. Not that he smoked, but who cared? At any rate, it was easier to get into a conversation with tradesmen at the Bar du Centre over a rollie than to ask, "So, are you a Hegel fan too?"

Loulou had realized that a friend was someone who laughed with her rather than at her. Only one person did that, and it was Marie-Jeanne. Well, horrible Luca did too, but he wasn't a friend, he was . . .

This thought triggered a cascade of images inside Loulou's head of her rubbing Luca's face with clumps of grass. He defended himself by rolling her over onto her back and kissing her. If only he would get angry again! She had come down with an incurable fever. To avoid thinking about Luca, she had become so hyperactive, such a workaholic, that even her parents could tell something was wrong.

From Marie-Jeanne's point of view, a friend was someone you could tell everything that was on your mind. She had only one such friend: the olive tree.

As for the olive tree, the wind was its friend, because it gave it a voice; the soil was its friend, because it was its home; and it also had the birds that perched on its swaying branches and brought it news from far and wide. It did however reserve its greatest love for this little girl. Not that she was so little anymore, especially not in terms of hyper-sensitivity: She could see love.

What a gift! the tree thought. *What a burden!*

When would she find out about what she knew?

Olive trees are the guardians of wisdom, etc. But the real question is: Why?

Trees and grasses and bushes, rocks and underground streams and the open oceans, live in constant contact with humans. They live in a different time zone from humans and are subject to the laws of infinite repetition. The mountains too are governed by timescales verging on eternal. This eternal presence supplies rock for building houses in which humans live such fleeting lives. But the stones remain.

The lifespan of an olive tree does not pass quite as slowly as that of a mountain. Its roots delve down into the earth, which tells them which paths the water has taken, drop by drop. Some of these drops fell long ago on Roman carts carrying women in uncomfortable bonnets before trickling into the ground, groping their way between stones and scree, and reaching the olive tree hundreds of years later.

This water tells stories of war and love, of crosses and fires, and how the world of men and women has changed. How they invented money and envy, how they built cities and wrote of an intact natural world they have pined for ever since.

The breeze and the storms and the winds and a flash of lightning: These too bear the scents of distant valleys and houses to the olive tree, and it pictures them with the silent eye of its ancient soul. It can smell the parlors and bedrooms and barns, the lives and meals and sleep of those who live there. From the breeze it can imagine the warmth and shape of the livestock, smell the milk and cheese and dried herbs, hear the prayers and voices, the whispered words of love and the unspoken desires. All these things the eloquent air tells the tree. It reveals how humans feel and which stories they recount to one another.

This eight-hundred-year-old olive tree knows every inch of these faraway valleys. It is familiar with their inhabitants' daytime routines and night thoughts. Thousands of years of life are archived in its trunk, interwoven and united with the tree.

The astonishing thing, as the olive tree knows, is that humans too have regular cycles. They are simply not as visible as the passing of the seasons. Recurrent decades of destruction cease and give way to regeneration and prosperity, and every period of wealth and well-being is followed by new devastation. That is how humans are. This is their natural law.

Even more than the wind and water, the olive tree likes the birds that settle on its branches. It listens, and they bring it news of villages and cities. The birds tell of laughter and music so similar to their language and yet so different.

This is how the tree watches, thinks, hears, and feels, storing up memories of worlds visible and invisible. This is how it knows about Marie-Jeanne's marvelous gift and knows what will happen.

19

The Alchemy of Books: Risks and Side Effects

Marie-Jeanne read everything she could get her hands on. Well, with one exception. Francis had skimmed through the book about hydraulic sensations with Jean Finkielkraut and together they had reached the following conclusions: First, they were too old for it; second, too prudish; third, their joints couldn't cope with it; and fourth, they couldn't let this piece of shoddy handiwork fall into the hands of a young girl.

Everything apart from that, though. She devoured *romans à l'eau de rose* whose covers showed renegade princes, revolutionaries, and pirates, who were generally pictured in torn blouses embracing women who gazed at them with adoring eyes. But she also read Camus and *A Guide to Modern Conjugation,* Jack Kerouac's *On the Road,* Aldous Huxley's *Brave New World* (which gave her nightmares), *The Catcher in the Rye,* and the letters of Ninon de Lenclos. She read Jules Verne and Johannes Mario Simmel, Sylvia Plath and *Waiting for Godot.* (This last book she found very rude, upon which Valérie explained to her in great detail that the play was a parable, a metaphor. This taught Marie-Jeanne that books sometimes don't say what they say but instead contain a hidden message behind the words. This seemed a complicated idea, but why not?)

She read *Jane Eyre* and *Stiller* (she guessed that Max Frisch's novel was one big sticky metaphor for a profound sadness). She read *Great Expectations* and *The Great Gatsby,* from which she learned that you don't have to be rich to bribe Love, which comforted her.

She might have been too young for some of this literature by conventional standards, but no one thought of keeping novels out of her hands. This may have been due to the fact that initially neither of her parents had a clue what was in these monster tomes. They were now happy for Marie-Jeanne to read aloud to them, and when they reached an explicit passage—usually in one of the "pink" books with a prince in an open-necked shirt—Elsa would remove the book from her hand, check the extract, and say, "Well, it doesn't clearly state what they're up to, but there are a few . . . what are they called? . . . Metaphors? There you go." Blushes all around, a frantic flicking of pages, and finally a strongly expressed desire from Elsa to return to the more difficult novels of Balzac and that despondent Russian. They didn't ambush the reader with a hail of metaphors such as the "urgent flood from his dagger-scepter."

Marie-Jeanne's education was only enhanced by these sessions, though not really in the traditional fashion. She also learned about the constellations in the night sky over Italian-speaking Switzerland, how the Japanese served tea, and how to blind a crocodile, make a sauce from the leaves of a rosebush, greet the queen of England, write the years in Chinese characters, and light a fire without matches.

The Picture of Dorian Gray encouraged Marie-Jeanne temporarily to give mirrors a wide berth. *Fahrenheit 451* made for an upsetting voyage into a bleak human future where there were no books, but she fell asleep with a burning desire to be able to narrate an entire novel from memory too. Just in case one day humans really did decide to ban literature from their lives to prevent rioting and regulate emotion and desire. In any case, pretty soon no one would be capable of reading more than a single paragraph before succumbing to brain pain.

But which novel should she memorize? Every time she thought she'd found her favorite book, she would open the next one and like it even better.

What was it Jean Finkielkraut, Petitpa's new pal, had said? "That's how to read—like a butterfly. It flutters around aimlessly until suddenly it stumbles upon an uncharted paradise. Don't listen to your teacher about what you should and shouldn't have read. Never be arrogant about certain types of books. Be a butterfly!"

So Marie-Jeanne butterflied her way through the gardens of poetry.

She read to Elsa as she was making lace, and afterward they would discuss the stories and the characters. They talked about this strange Monsieur Kafka who had plunged Elsa into confusion. The ordeals Gregor was subjected to in *The Metamorphosis* broke her heart, especially the fact that his own mother treated him like vermin.

Elsa didn't notice it at first, but with every book she moved closer to an inner equilibrium. She wouldn't have been herself if she didn't mask her transformation into a milder fusspot from the outside world. She did, however, start to neglect her former habit of putting people's noses out of joint.

It was she who came up with the idea of sewing fabric covers to protect the books. This had the additional advantage of preventing anyone from identifying at first glance what another person was reading.

Elsa had also spent one afternoon pondering those hydraulic contortions, but she had then dismissed it all as an overly strenuous means of pursuing pleasure. All the same, they did offer some interesting inspiration from which, who knew, Francis might benefit at some later date.

The book received a pretty fabric cover with a delightful embroidered likeness of the Virgin Mary on it. Once, glancing in the mirror on the old sideboard, Francis caught his wife flashing him a furtive smile, and he stored that smile away inside him. Since then, he had often turned around to see if he could catch another of those tender gazes she prayed would fall to the floor unseen.

There was a little part of her, though, that did in fact want him to intercept her longing glances. This feeling was new to her. New, light, and bright. She wasn't falling in love with her husband, was she?

The bookabus was soon as much a part of everyday life as TV series, farmers converting their barns and cowsheds into holiday *gîtes,* and the summer camps where young people from the gray cities soaked up some proper sunshine and longed to lose their bothersome virginity.

Among lavender beds and in olive groves and goat sheds,

sitting by the fireside or on the outside toilet behind the chicken coop, people read *Papillon, Viper in the Fist,* the Claudine series, and *Bonjour Tristesse.*

They learned about life, drinking it in with a thousand eyes. They were rejuvenated. They grew wiser. They knew happiness as only those who listen to themselves and smile do. That first wild summer of books changed them.

To the horror of all "decent women" (a widespread but nameless authority), Martine, the second daughter of the baker in Nyons, had her hair cropped short. Gérard, the mayor's elder son, grew his hair long ("like a hippie/terrorist/anarchist," etc.). It was a time of upheaval, and since books offered some precious tips to get a tremulous nation to dance, these two youngsters thought they would bring down a few barriers with their hairstyles.

Who was to blame? Hmm. Some people thought it was Hermann Hesse's fault, others accused Jack Kerouac, and a third group had that madman Scott Fitzgerald and *Tender Is the Night* in their sights. And who was their head henchman? Francis Meurienne, with his intensifying reputation as a harmless, smiling saboteur who boosted the demand for books with discreet fabric covers.

When he was asked about this haircut revolution, Francis quoted a line from Seneca that he had picked up from Colette: "People are more concerned about the outer finery of their heads than about their inner order."

Jean Finkielkraut, the writer with writer's block, was impressed. It was quite something to be able to quote Seneca *and* replace a spark plug. That was the kind of man he wanted to be one day. For some time, his worldview had been taking a bit of a battering, and the bright light and colors of the south came flooding through the gaps and cracks. Jean's intellectual ambitions and the more physical aspects of his character sat down together and made peace.

Meanwhile, the cobbler's leathery heart had been tenderized by Angélique's adventures and he began to dream of shoes that might carry people out of their everyday routines. He whispered his ideas to his wife, Violetta, at night when he thought she was sleeping. She wasn't, though, and she listened and fell in love with him for real. Their dream destination, America, was a little too far away, so the two of them drove to the seaside for the very first time. They had a picnic of bread and rillettes on the beach, washed down with a bottle of rosé they'd left in the surf to cool. It was so much more joyous than their wedding day had been. As they watched the slow pulse of the dazzling white stars up above, they agreed that they had never been happier. It was as if the sky were below them and they were sailing over it with their backs to the sand and their eyes riveted on its depths.

Luc le Marseillais was persuaded to allow the Bar du Centre to serve as a returns counter for the mobile library. Resting his elbows on the bar, he read Dostoyevsky and stopped losing money on the horses and drinking away his subsequent shame. Death came to him several decades later than Fate had suggested it would. To which Wonder remarked: Well, you can never count on me, only hope in me.

At some stage, thanks to the mobile library, Jean—the most unlikely candidate—discovered the secret of the southern lights. Well, almost.

Jean had relocated from Paris to Nyons for two reasons, the first being vanity. The merest glimpse of Simone de Beauvoir's turban bobbing past would make Parisians swoon as they sat sipping coffee on a Saint Germain café terrace. Jean had therefore donned similar headgear in a bid to make an impression, but he merely looked like his aunt Elsbetha, who herself looked like a beturbaned Louis de Funès. His hope had been that he would be a star in southern France, rather than just another author, and that he would bear this heavy responsibility with modesty and diffident pride.

True, there was that science fiction author, René Barjavel. Oh, and Jean Giono. Yes, all right, so there was Marcel Pagnol too. Jean could ignore them, though.

His second reason for moving away from the Seine was that he had a profound and distressing sense that he was being cheated out of life. In the metro and while he walked on the pavement, the stones and asphalt in between seemed to cut him off from the grass and the earth with its many scents, and Paris had become so fast and loud and self-important. All the styles and needs and trends; everyone always wondering: What's the new fashion, the newer fashion, the newest fashion?

Ever since de Gaulle had been succeeded by Pompidou and then died, Jean had ceased to feel at home in Paris. He had longed to be in *la France profonde* and enjoy a somewhat idealized country life far from the hectic antics of the times in age-old Provence where the brightness and the blue skies would cure him of the cold northern light. This was what he wanted to write about. He wanted to let the nation breathe in a book whose working title was *The Forgotten Present*.

The things intellectuals undertake when they reach a certain age and realize that they have lived inside their head too much and inside their body too little. In addition, Jean was sick of being cold and wanted to get drunk in the warm embrace of one glorious night. He was also desperate to meet a woman who would at least be bold enough to hold hands with him. It had been such a long time, and he guessed he was probably too out of practice for anything more.

How Monsieur Finkielkraut forgot how to love

Having been the class grind and something of an outcast because his sense of honor forbade him to go along with the other boys' stupid pranks, Jean Finkielkraut had been under the romantic illusion that writing was his one and only passion.

However, sixty years had now passed and still that peculiar alchemy did not make him happy. However beautifully he described his own life in words, the loneliness would come flooding back as soon as he stopped typing. He felt like a mere bystander who was never invited to join in, combined with a deep-rooted sense of not being handsome enough. No woman would ever choose to dream about him; he would only ever appear in her feverish nightmares. His head was too full and his heart was too timid. The only thing that really inflamed his passions was a first-rate argument conducted with all guns blazing.

He had slunk away with his tail between his legs instead of learning to live with his true love, who was probably at this very moment, for the two thousand one hundred and tenth time, setting the table for one before raising her wineglass alone to an invisible man she imagined was sitting opposite her and for whom she had gone to such lengths. She had made herself beautiful for him, she had cooked for him, and later she would put on a tango record and read something from her favorite book by Simone Weil. She never shied away from hurling herself headlong into an explosive debate on any subject and making full use of her abundant knowledge and rich vocabulary.

And yet here he sat, the oblivious, unhappy simpleton, crafting grand alphabet soup for no one in particular.

Every morning Jean would write and then wait for Francis to come for lunch so he could treat him to one of his runny desserts and read to him from his newest literary opus.

"Very good!" Francis would say.

This was a man who read Sartre and Kant, Jean thought, congratulating himself (although Francis had recently discovered Jules Verne, whose works he greatly preferred).

On the morning Jean had his near-revelation about love, the glow, and the greatest secret of all, he had composed the following lines on his portable typewriter:

Among lavender beds, in olive groves and goat sheds, sitting by the fireside or on the outside toilet behind the chicken coop, people read Papillon, *the Claudine series, and* Bonjour Tristesse. *The Philis Mobile Library run by former deliveryman and bric-a-brac collector Francis Meurienne had made life in the valley of Nyons sweeter. All of a sudden, there were a thousand new words for people to whisper to one another when the indigo hour came, and first hands and then lips met. Confessions were couched in these new words. Letters were penned, plans were forged, and the ocean of books across which we struck out with that mobile library carried us away to the uncharted territories of our own minds.*

"Damn and blast," the muse at Jean's shoulder exclaimed. She had accidentally dropped a metaphorical bomb on his manuscript.

Only those who had no one to love set their books aside. They felt a faint burning sensation in their chest and then, slowly, a thin column of yearning rose up from each of their rooms into the night sky. A glowing, aching beam of light.

"Where are you?" it whispered.

The whisperings rose up on the breeze to the top of the mountains, where the mistral seized them with its mighty hand and swept them southward to the sea.

"Where are you?" a voice would suddenly ask from close by. A voice out of nowhere that could only be felt, never heard, sometimes as a pang in the heart, sometimes as a burning sensation in the chest.

Nice! Now for a little glass of rosé. Jean was pleased.

I was not.

20

Jean Finkielkraut's Muse Goes to the Pictures

I leaned over Jean's shoulder and read the latest products of his imagination for a second time.

Dearie me! It wasn't good. It really wasn't good. For starters, the author didn't realize that in a fit of insight he had been writing about himself, about a desire that he disregarded and the voices of faraway lovers he had never heard.

Who was it who coined the phrase "Love makes you blind"?

"*Plato, darling. Plato,*" whispered Intelligence.

He did? What insulting slander. The truth is that humans don't require my intervention to trudge through life blind and deaf; they're quite capable of doing that by themselves. In actual fact, I'm the one who opens their eyes. Only the loving can see the most wonderful aspects of other people, because eyes are of no use—it takes a different sense, a part of the body that doesn't feature in any atlas of human anatomy. Curses and double curses, couldn't Finkielkraut write about that for once?

"Am I to take that as my mission?"

"Grrr."

"Are we perhaps feeling a little tense?"

"Yes, we are!"

"Would you like to talk about it?"

Muses are peculiar creatures—half guardian angel, half walking disaster. They show artists the hidden paths that lead ever deeper into their souls. But every now and then they just abandon them down in the gorges and caverns and chasms, and pop out for a swim or go and watch a movie. They do keep listening, though.

Given what was happening, it was time to speak out. Was I in crisis?

What do you think?

Love in crisis

It had begun with not being able to touch Marie-Jeanne, and now this obscure scribbler—already one of the toughest nuts I'd ever had to crack—was prying into my activities with his typewriter in a way that verged on wanton demystification. What's more, he was too stupid to figure out that he needed to do a little less literature and a bit more living.

"Don't worry," the muse said, "it'll all turn out fine."

"What do you mean? It's been going downhill for centuries. It really was better in the old days. Then, unlike in this horribly unmagical century, I was regarded neither as pure emotion nor as glorious salvation. There were splendid, authentic times when I was one among the following list of elements: water, fire, air, earth, metal, love, and hate."

"Wow," the muse said.

"Imagine that! I'm like a volcanic eruption, as crucial as the invention of fire in the genesis of civilization and sensuality."

"I get your point. So you feel undervalued?" When did muses start majoring in psychology?

"There used to be teachings about which element corresponded to each individual, along with its strengths and weaknesses. They are still ubiquitous in China today, but love and hate have been stripped of their status as elements. Wouldn't it have been nice, though, to have a love pig to place alongside the fire crow, the earth horse, and the water buffalo?"

"Absolutely," the muse hastened to remark.

It isn't nice, I can tell you, to be demoted to a lower category, all because various philosophers and churchmen are embarrassed about me and haughtily overestimate my revolutionary, creative, destructive, inspiring, supernatural influence on the course of human history. That's just as true of Hate, but Hate can find its own advocates!

"I feel as if people don't take me seriously nowadays. But no, I don't want to talk about it."

"Oops," the muse said. "Let's pretend I never asked, okay?"

What Jean Finkielkraut had written about me was accurate, even though otherwise he had as little knowledge of my character as a goat does of Kandinsky's paintings.

"Could you burn that, please?" I whispered to the author, and he blinked a few times, looked around in bafflement, and took another sip of Bandol rosé.

What now?

"Can I do anything more to help, darling?" the muse asked, stroking the back of Jean's neck.

"Would you be so kind as to make him burn those pages and forget he ever wrote them?"

"What do I get in return?"

"Some peace. Who knows what might pop into his mind about muses?"

"No one believes anything they read in books."

"Books are the sole repository of authenticity."

"But peace is so terribly uncreative!" the muse said.

"Precisely my point. Let's watch him go to war with himself and then write about something else."

"Darling," the muse commented, "that's far too complicated for me." She ran her fingers over Jean's eyes and soon afterward he furrowed his brow, pulled the sheet of paper out of the typewriter, crumpled it up, and tossed it into a corner.

Then the muse went to the movies. "*The Gendarme Gets Married,*" she said meaningfully as she flitted off.

All right, I thought.

Jean wasn't aware that very close to where he was fretting—so close that he passed her every market day—lived a woman who thought of him each time she dined alone and imagined that he was there at the table with her: a Monsieur Finkielkraut she'd never met. If he had known that, he would have written a different novel. It wouldn't have been called *The Forgotten Present* but *The Idiot: A Modern*

Retelling. Or he would have packed up his typewriter, his favorite pencil, a bottle of wine, and a change of underwear and finally embarked on his life. He wouldn't have needed to go far.

"What am I going to do with you?" I muttered. "You traitor to love."

To some people I must have seemed unhinged.

21

A Small Fold in Time and What Happened There

The bookabus was thriving like an Italian ice-cream parlor in midsummer. The first wild bookish autumn was followed by a literary winter as the evenings began to close in. How wonderful they felt sitting by the fire, reading books, feeling the heat on their cheeks and tummies, its glow running up their spines. How sweet to turn in for the night with their heads full of images and fragrances, cradled by the scents of the Far East and rocked by the gentle swell of a translucent sea.

Spring tiptoed in and out, giving way to the next boiling-hot summer. Elsa's cookbook came out in print. Marie-Jeanne grew so quickly that her legs were soon too long for her to ride Fino, so Francis bought her a good-natured mare from the Camargue called Napoléonne.

Now the third mobile librarian, albeit an apprentice, Marie-Jeanne rode through the hills delivering books. She wore her hair in a long plait again and had a special book harness fitted to her saddle. She was known as the *gardienne des livres,* in reference to the riders who watched over the bulls and horses of the Camargue, because she liked to wear a bull runner's costume—leather trousers, a white shirt, a weatherproof black jacket, a knotted necktie, and a Camargue cowboy's hat. Her eyes flashed sky blue in her suntanned face. She loved this *lunel* hat, which sat so snugly on her head and helped focus her thoughts.

She had a lot on her mind. It felt as if she still didn't have the key to open up what she had learned about the world so far. About people, things, books, the glow, and the gods, of which there were clearly an almost infinite number.

Valérie had told her, "You already have every god, every hell, and every heaven inside you."

"Goodness me," Elsa had cried, banging her fist on the table. "Now, that would explain a lot of things."

Marie-Jeanne wondered how people came to be the way they were. How they changed very quickly while they were young and then increasingly slowly as they aged. She considered what would happen when she turned thirteen. She was waiting to discover her glow, but so far it hadn't appeared, even though other people got theirs at the very latest when they became teenagers.

Where would it appear? How would it feel? Would life seem bigger? Would she be a grown-up, and what did it mean to be a grown-up, to know all the things that adults didn't tell children? Or to forget what she had known as a child?

She and Napoléonne rode along paths used for driving sheep and goats up to and down from the summer pastures, wending their way between gorse bushes and wild olive groves, past truffle oaks and dreamy abandoned vineyards. She also rode along the banks of the river Eygues every day, and at a shallow spot she would allow her horse to splash around in the water. As a sign of gratitude toward her two-legged friend, the mare would press her soft, downy nostrils against Marie-Jeanne's neck and blow until she giggled.

Such wonderful days.

She looked up at the clouds to see what the weather was doing, and the scents of the earth would tell her if summer was on its way out. On her mountain rides she met ibex (they didn't glow), griffon vultures (they did), and timid wildcats (no way; no glowing).

As another year of the library passed, I grew increasingly desperate because it was proving impossible to place the intended mark on Marie-Jeanne.

Luca kissed a girl called Béatrice, and Loulou kissed a boy called Andrés, even if these were only harmless confirmation pecks that left both Loulou and Luca both confused and relieved. It was easy. Not incredibly hard, as it would be with . . .

"Things would never have worked out between me and Luca anyway," Loulou said.

"It would never have come to anything with Loulou anyway," Luca said.

"Besides, I don't think about him anymore," Loulou said.

"Besides, I don't think about her anymore," Luca said.

"Not for one second," they both said.

I wanted to give Marie-Jeanne a good shake.

"So do I, but it's totally illogical," Logic said.

We thought about celebrating this rare moment of consensus but couldn't agree how, so we went our own ways, scratching our heads.

"Those children are up to nonsense. Thoroughgoing nonsense," the olive tree said, but unfortunately, the only creature that heard its words was a vulture who couldn't have given a damn.

This was a few years before Jacques Chirac was appointed prime minister and the lavender fields went into mourning at the news of Marcel Pagnol's death. There were three TV channels and you needed to ingratiate yourself with a neighbor to watch Bernard Pivot's show *Apostrophes,* on which he chatted to authors about books and usually about wine as well. There was room for everything from gardening guides to contemporary novels and philosophical treatises as well as pirate romances, and Pivot's enthusiasm for literature of all kinds caught on across the country. It became as natural to discuss the most recent novels as it was to talk about the Tour de France, the weather, or the "higher-ups" whose political choices bamboozled those "down below." Books had gone from being the preserve of the bourgeois elite to a common good. At the hairdresser's or at the market, it was as common to hear the words "Have you read ——'s new book?" as it was to catch someone saying, "Good heavens, this weather makes my legs ache!"

In 1971 Marie-Jeanne turned thirteen. She kept checking under the covers on the night before her birthday to see if it had appeared. She got out of bed again and peered into the tiny mirror above the washbasin. It had been the right height for her when she started school, but now all she could see was her belly button. She twisted her body into impossible positions and even inspected the backs of her elbows. Nothing. No glow.

She felt even wider awake than before. A thousand cogs whirred away inside her head, spinning slowly, but their humming rose in pitch as they gradually worked themselves loose.

Maybe it would only come while she was asleep?

"Very funny," she said out loud.

Should she ask Elsa to pat her to sleep with a wooden spoon? She tried to fall asleep by rolling her eyes up under her eyelids, but they kept slipping back down again. She thought about how Valérie had never revealed who she used to live with. And how exhausted Loulou was from arguing with Luca, the only outcome being a gift of a beetle once, until she had eventually decided to love someone else instead called . . . Damn, was it so important to remember his name? She thought about how both Luca and Loulou each continued to profess that they didn't care one jot about the other.

But first, couldn't you just make love happen? And second, couldn't you . . .

She fell asleep at last before she could complete this thought.

Seven hours later, before she even opened her eyes, she thought about the glow. Off with the covers!

22

A Girl Goes up the Mountain

Nothing. Even standing barefoot in front of the mirror and contorting herself to examine every inch of skin, Marie-Jeanne couldn't spot anything.

When Elsa brought in her birthday cake, a tarte Tatin made with Reinette apples: Nothing happened.

When Francis gave her a penknife, a Laguiole blade with a handle made from a mammoth's tooth ("Just imagine, a sixteen-year-old blacksmith came up with the idea of a prehistoric Laguiole!"): still nothing.

Nothing happened that morning in late March. Nada. Zero. Zilch. Who knew, maybe she'd been forgotten, or maybe what the priest had said was true: Not everyone had an epiphany, and she was now the barefoot monster. She felt a fluttering in the pit of her stomach the size of a sparrow. The fluttering was so frenetic that she couldn't even manage to blow out the candles because the sparrow was growing bigger and bigger, and there was no room left for air for her to breathe.

. . .

I stood facing her but still I couldn't touch her. It was distressing.

"Is everything all right?" Francis asked.

"I'm not sure I really exist."

"Hmm. You'll soon be a grown woman," Elsa said, her expression less sullen than usual. "The child is moving out, and the woman is moving in, but you might feel a bit absent while that process is going on. Do you have any questions about this or any other, um, girly issues?"

"I'd rather not talk about it," Marie-Jeanne said.

"Thank God," Francis mumbled.

"Actually . . ."

"Um, I need to see a man about a horse." Francis fled the kitchen.

When he had shut the door, Elsa asked, "What is it you want to know?"

"How do you tell you're a grown-up?"

Elsa looked out the window, as if the air might have a message for her. The same air that no longer fit in Marie-Jeanne, however many deep breaths she took.

Elsa gave her answer to the air. "When you start to miss the wonders you believed in as a child."

"Oh," the girl said, "that's . . ." *Probably the worst thing imaginable.*

What had she expected? That Elsa would say, "Oh, you can tell from the little glow that appears. It's as natural as stubble or periods. It appears just like that; you don't have to wait, it just happens. By the way, isn't it right there on the top of your eyelid? No wonder you didn't spot it!"

"Marie-Jeanne?"

"Yes?"

"Don't worry, everything will find its place—including you." She gently stroked the girl's cheek before, on reflection, patting it harder. "And make sure I don't catch you hiding in the straw with one of those boys before it's time, do you hear me?" She wagged her finger.

Ha ha, very funny, thought Marie. If it was as bad as she thought it would be, she'd rather spend her whole lifetime in the straw with a pack of wildcats.

She tried to regulate her breathing to manage her shortness of breath. It was hard getting dressed, because what for? They'd be waiting for her at school. There would be the usual lighted candle on the table to celebrate her birthday, and everyone would stand up and sing a song. It would be horrible. She didn't want a song. She didn't want to stand in front of a group of thirteen- and fourteen-year-olds, spitting fireworks from their toes and hair and bitten fingernails.

She wanted to be like everyone else. She wanted to glow too.

She saddled up Napoléonne and decided she wouldn't go to school, nor would she tell anyone about her decision except Meeny, Miny, Moe, and Tictac.

"We're with you," the cats said, and went their own ways. Tictac wagged his tail appreciatively.

Marie-Jeanne rode along the narrow and silent paths to Aimée Claudel's *mazet.* No one would see her and ask her questions that she wouldn't be able to answer at all diplomatically today.

I followed her because it had to be possible to find out why I couldn't put my mark on this child.

. . .

"I need to ask you something!" Marie-Jeanne whispered to the olive tree from her perch high in its branches.

Oh dear, the ancient colossus thought. So today was the day. It had feared this day yet knew that it would come around whether it feared it or not.

The girl jumped down from the branches and scratched the tree's back out of habit.

"It's my thirteenth birthday today."

"How lovely it is that you exist."

"Hmm," she said.

"What did you want to ask me?"

(We should remember that the olive tree could only give answers to the right questions. It couldn't just rattle off fundamental truths, which didn't always facilitate important conversations.)

"Is it true about the glow?"

"What do *you* think?"

"I think it is."

"Then it is."

"What if I'd said it wasn't?"

"Then it would still be true."

"It can't depend entirely on me whether people who glow, glow."

"All I can tell you, Marie-Jeanne, is that they glow for you to see. You are the element who decides to make something of the glow or not."

"I'm not very good at making something of it. I don't even know what it means or if I'm just imagining it to make myself feel important. Maybe I'm crazy and no one's telling me. Maybe I've fallen off my horse and am lying in a forgotten room at the end of a corridor, powerless to wake up from a dream I mistake for my life."

"We can rule that out."

"Look at me, though. Can *you* see anything on me?"

"I can see a lot of things," the tree said. "Generosity. Altruism. Attentiveness. I see an extraordinary person. I wish I could be with you wherever you go in life and watch you becoming who you will be, but I have to stay here. And it hurts me when you are sad, but then I think of you. You must never forget that when you're sad, I'm thinking about you. I am with you."

She hugged its trunk. She wept quietly, and it cursed the fact that it was just a tree with no arms to embrace her.

"What should I do?" she asked.

The olive tree could answer that question at least. "Ride to the top of the highest mountain and wait for nightfall. You will understand everything then."

Now the only sound the tree made was to rustle its leaves, however much Marie-Jeanne begged it to tell her whether it meant the highest mountain in the area, the Alps, or the world.

Before she could ponder for too long whether she had been talking with an olive tree or merely to herself, Marie-Jeanne wiped away her tears, blew her nose, went home, and got out a map she had found in her grandmother's house.

The nearest high mountain was the 4,390-foot Montagne de la Lance, and the highest in the area was the 6,263-foot Mont Ventoux. She could tackle the Alps some other time.

"Okay then," she said, packing up everything she would need for her grand tour. She planned to be back by midnight and was prepared for a good telling-off by Elsa. She directed Napoléonne's hooves toward the sky.

From the summit of the Montagne de la Lance she could see the whole of the Drôme and Provence laid out before her with their hills and mountains and peaks and crags. She got off the horse, left it to graze on a few cowering herbs, and twirled slowly on her own axis. The Lance's crown was bald except for a few feeble fir saplings and scree that had been shoved around by the wind. As she rotated faster and faster, the folds of the rocky mountains began to look more and more as if they were moving, like waves. As if they were part of a terrestrial ocean.

"What now?" she asked Napoléonne.

All she got by way of reply was the sound of the horse's chomping jaws.

"You're right. Now we wait for nightfall."

She took the saddle off the mare's back, wrapped herself in a blanket, and leaned against the leather until the ground flipped and the horizon was higher than the sun. The countryside was dusted with a fine red-gold sheen. Then it went blue, and finally black.

Marie-Jeanne waited.

Was this the right mountain? Why was she following the instructions of an olive tree whose words probably only she could interpret, even if the old folk sometimes claimed that an olive grove was the library of life? They tended to say such things, though, when they were desperate for some peace and quiet from their families, the daily routine, and the throbbing worries inside their heads. It was then that they would retreat with a bottle of Château Something-or-Other into the silent orchards and listen to the melodies of their winged brothers, the cicadas.

The wind was getting cooler and the stars came out. Still Marie-Jeanne waited.

23

The Secret of the Southern Lights

The evening breeze crept under Marie-Jeanne's blanket, and its cool hand made her shiver. Napoléonne lay down somewhat awkwardly, and she huddled closer to the surf-white flank of the large, warm, breathing horse.

She shut her eyes and opened them again. The world lay still and silent beneath her. The loneliness began. Sleep would not bring her its peacefulness, when Morpheus covers our eyes with his great hand; some people are unable to close them under its weight because they feel such a tugging sensation inside. This tugging kindles a spark, a light that gently detaches itself from the slumbering twilight and escapes into the silence of the night.

Marie-Jeanne waited and watched. She sobbed a little but then, as something inside her began to slip and slide slowly into a still-inexpressible understanding, an acquiescence, she stopped crying.

As I sat next to her, I would have loved to hold her suntanned hand with its light pink fingernails. I would have liked to tell her how special she was to the people she met. How much better they always felt afterward.

And while I wrestled with my wishes and Marie-Jeanne rubbed away the tracks of her tears from her sweet face, they came. Miracles are always possible, and sometimes they happen in the darkest places.

Along the southern edge, where the land met the sea, tiny dots of light pierced holes in night's black mantle. Lights coming on in distant rooms and houses?

In a sense they were. Except that these lights were not stealing out from lampshades and candlesticks into the velvety darkness but spiraling up from people's chests and earlobes and fingers and shoulders to cover the great distance to her. Gossamer lights twinkling up into the ether on delicate threads. They came up from the south first and then made their way up into the valleys. Higher and higher they rose, up to the stars.

"Do you see them, Napoléonne?" Marie-Jeanne whispered.

A snort. A nod.

Four eyes on top of the Montagne de la Lance. Four eyes and me, foolish Love.

And below us lights soaring up. Lanterns. Stars shooting up quickly, quickly after their sojourn on Earth, lengthening into delicate strands of such incredible strength . . . They glowed.

When these threads were caught by a gust of wind, they seemed to fray, and the lights swirled and dissipated. They were blown toward the sea or up into the mountains; they swarmed upriver on the eddying air or rose ever higher until they disappeared among the glittering stars, adding their numbers to the Milky Way and making the whole firmament sparkle.

Marie-Jeanne got to her feet. She stretched her arms out horizontally and spun around, and all around her she saw the lights. A glowing. Glittering strands reaching out farther and farther until they crisscrossed the peaks and the horizon and encompassed all the sky in between.

Oh! Now one light spark had reached the summit of the Montagne de la Lance, swirling up on the wind, then tumbling down and dancing in ever-decreasing circles toward Marie-Jeanne.

A searching, inviting light.

She held out her hand, turned it so the palm was facing upward, and opened her fingers, as if she were attempting to lure a little bird. After a momentary hesitation, the tiny southern light settled, exhausted, on her cupped hand.

Marie-Jeanne slowly leaned forward and pulled the blanket over her head. Now she cradled the southern light in both hands—a droplet of eternity in the chalice of her fingers. She closed her eyes and listened to it.

You will see my beauty. My eyes. The way I look at you. You will love it when I put my hand in yours as we go to sleep.

Where are you?

What were you like when you were young? How long ago is that? Can you still feel, with fear and joy in your tummy and the lights of your very first night on your own in your eyes, when, out of nothing, you felt a sudden longing for an individual you didn't know?

Were you by the sea, as I was?

Where were you when love wove its spell around you?
Where are you, and will you find me?

The light rose up from her hand and sailed away.

Marie-Jeanne spent that whole night on the mountaintop. She watched the dots and strands of light and she knew that these were the glow, which set out from someone's mouth or shoulders, toes or hair, or even the fourth buttonhole from the top of someone's shirt to seek out the person to whom it was attached.

When daybreak came, the lights would return home and roll themselves up under the person's heart, in the very spot where she herself felt a pang of emptiness—and she filled it with other people's pain.

Southern lights. That's what she would call these Morse code messages of yearning and their long-standing connection with their unknown counterparts. If only they could find them—or at least know where they were to be found!

Marie-Jeanne recited under her breath the verse she had transcribed from that wonderful old book at Madame Colette's house. It felt like a thousand years ago, when she was still a child. She had ceased to be one an hour ago.

The minute I heard my first love story,
I started looking for you, not knowing
how blind that was.
Lovers don't finally meet somewhere.
They're in each other all along.

She pieced together what she knew and what she believed and eventually she had only one remaining question: "And what about me?"

As the darkness thinned and yielded to day, as the lights wended their way back to the dreaming bodies of people who would soon open their eyes and sense a nameless pain below their hearts, Marie-Jeanne rode slowly—very slowly—home. She was scared of the answer to her question.

I wanted to ask her for forgiveness. Maybe life would be better without me. Without love. Humans would like one another and no more. People could stay together or choose not to, and no one would have to run into the jagged prongs of unrequited or lost love. All the hooks and tines a heart encounters—a name, a make of car, a fragrance, another person's laughter. That peaceful moment before falling asleep when the yearning comes flooding back. Or waking up to another day without him, another day without her.

Wasted life.

And so the day the olive tree had feared the most came to pass

"I don't have a southern light," Marie-Jeanne told the tree. She hadn't bothered to dismount from her horse, and the olive tree had never seen her face so close to its silvery sprigs before.

In her eyes it saw a glimmer, but it was not the one she longed to have. It was her view of the world. She was almost like Love itself, like me. She spied the essence of every person and every object, but of course she wasn't me. She wasn't a goddess or an element; she was a young woman who could see Love.

She was capable of recognizing the southern lights and the misery of the lonely.

What was the tree to say? It had never lied to Marie-Jeanne and it wasn't going to start now, so it kept quiet.

"But if I don't have one, and I fear I never will, how is anyone supposed to find me? With whom will I ever be united? Who am I supposed to love if there is no one marked out for me? Does that mean that no one in the world loves me? That there's no one I can call my own?"

"That's correct," the tree said.

Marie-Jeanne hung her head. "Very well," she said. "Fine."

The situation really wasn't fine, so how come this brave young woman, who radiated such kindness and respect and brought so much compassion and happiness into the world, said it?

The budding young woman was no longer looking at the tree but staring vacantly into the distance. Then the transformed Marie-Jeanne Claudel, who was ready to face up to anything now, even though she was afraid of spending an endless series of endless days without any hope of ever finding love, said, "Love hates going to waste. I don't have to be loved, and if that is how it has to be, I can love those who love. The value of life is nothing but the meaning that you choose."

I covered my eyes with my hands so I wouldn't have to witness this scene. The tree also wished that it could do more than run its sunlit fingers over her face. It started to rain, and the tree wept.

24

Marie-Jeanne Chooses Her Vocation

"Where have you been?"

"All over."

"What were you doing there?"

"Nothing."

"Can you even imagine how worried we've been?"

"Yes, but I haven't spent much time imagining it in detail."

Since Elsa didn't know how to respond to this—"Oh yeah? So what was so urgent that *mademoiselle* had to stay away for two whole days, eh?" or "Who is this strange girl with a plait anyway?" or "It doesn't matter. The main thing is that you're back safe and sound, with all your arms and legs intact. Have a piece of this stinking cheese and see if you feel like telling *it* what's going on"—she said nothing and sat down again in bewilderment.

Elsa and Francis had been through hell, but they had discovered a little patch of heaven there. The first night, through her tears, Elsa had confided that Marie-Jeanne was the most wonderful thing in her life and that she wasn't willing to lose such a wonder just yet and probably never would be. Even if she wasn't the girl's biological mother, she longed to be her real mother, because the girl contained everything that was good about Elsa, however tiny that "everything" might be. Even if it was no larger than an olive.

Francis had embraced her, and she had melted into his arms.

This patch of heaven lasted precisely five minutes before she reverted to being her normal prickly self.

When the two of them started scolding the girl again—Elsa very loudly, Francis very gently—Marie-Jeanne continued her musings as if she were deep underwater and these two dear people were far-off boats, their keels gliding past a long way above her head.

She sat there in the kitchen and watched the glowing southern lights uniting her parents. Never before had they been so apparent, sparkling and spraying from Francis's boat-shaped mouth and Elsa's clever fingers.

Elsa's glow shone whenever she complained about Francis's lack of paternal severity ("Say something, for goodness' sake!").

They're constantly spinning threads around each other, Marie-Jeanne thought, *and they don't even realize.* The absurdity and beauty of it all made her laugh. She knew that if Francis ever had the crazy idea of kissing his wife's hands—every single one of those enterprising, searching, yearning fingers that channeled her love into all the things she created—he would get a bigger shock than he had bargained for.

But first things first: That was all still in the future.

The two of them talked as Marie-Jeanne sank ever deeper into a sea of thoughts. *I'm condemned to sleep alone, a lifetime long. I will be the only one to touch my face. A lifetime long.*

She was scared, but her life mission was to make lovers

who couldn't see each other visible to each other. She breathed out at length, emptying her lungs entirely. *It is what it is.* A bird learning to fly had first to let itself fall.

"Petitpa," she said, "can I take over market days in Nyons with the bookabus?"

Francis nodded. He was relieved that she could still talk, because the last half an hour had been like an endless odyssey across a silent sea. He would have agreed to anything.

Vocation (n.)

Professional writers know all about this. If you stay quite silent and quite still, you will hear something calling inside you. A story, or a scene from a story. Or a strange, vague sense of "Oh, that might make a good story," its outline just about discernible through a pane of frosted glass. So you respond by sitting down and attempting to pull this story out from inside you as it whimpers to be set free and loved. And you don't stop; however long it takes and however often you cannot hear yourself above the noise of the outside world, you are not rude enough to interrupt so that you can actually hear yourself.

Marie-Jeanne heard something inside herself and answered the call. Maybe too quickly. Maybe not. Maybe she had misunderstood the voice, or the voice hadn't articulated its message properly.

During the summer holidays Marie-Jeanne managed the bookabus from seven A.M. to one P.M. on the Place des Arcades in Nyons (while Napoléonne waited under a parasol nearby). She had a plan whose imponderables she didn't wish to think about too hard because there were so many of them. She told herself to tackle one problem after another, not all of them at once.

It was only fitting that she set up the bookabus between approximately seven hundred multicolored varieties of tomatoes, apricots, cherries, strawberries, lettuces, Roquefort-flavored salamis, gracefully ripened cheeses, eggs still warm from the nest, and wooden dishes brimming with olives. Books deserved to be part of this rich spread. In fact, the real question was how anyone could ever have thought that literature could be separated from any of the other staple foods of life.

Géraldine Châtelet was a proud woman as well as a book addict, and she treated Marie-Jeanne with the same amiable distance with which she treated everyone else. She took good care to hide the fact that her broom and the girl's behind-and-below had experienced an unedifying coming together three years ago.

She usually borrowed books by Simone Weil (of course), but so far she hadn't treated Marie-Jeanne to a glimpse of her southern light. Who knew, maybe the glowing thread only unraveled when its beneficiary was in the vicinity? Or perhaps it led to someone in Paris or Buenos Aires (more likely, as the birthplace of tango)? How was Géraldine supposed to follow it there and persuade the recipient to board a ship and travel back with her to a remote valley in the Drôme?

Anyway, one problem at a time.

As Madame Châtelet walked away across the square today,

Marie-Jeanne saw her glow begin to pulsate gently, then uncoil. It was her southern light!

Napoléonne gave a snort.

"Shh!" the girl said. "And don't stare at her."

The horse and the girl followed what happened next out of the corners of their eyes. The little thread bobbed up and down before darting forward, winding its lengthening strands around the plane tree in the middle of the market square, and then creeping softly across the flagstones to old Maurice Poulard's cheese stall. He was the man who had made the analogy between lemon trees on the Champs-Élysées and book-reading daughters, but it had fallen a bit flat.

Could he really be . . . ?

No, it wasn't Maurice Poulard. Jean Finkielkraut was standing there. The unicorn glow on his forehead caught hold of the thread and they intertwined.

"Not Buenos Aires after all," Marie-Jeanne whispered. "Géraldine Châtelet and Jean Finkielkraut."

Two southern lights had found each other. Now their owners merely had to notice.

25

The Impossibility of Love at First Resighting

At this delicate stage, it might be good to provide a short update on Jean Finkielkraut, who was bending over a range of goat cheeses of varying ripeness, undecided as to which to buy, and therefore didn't notice the love of his life walk past with a wicker shopping basket in her hand.

Jean had recently published an acclaimed "provincial novel," which *Le Figaro* had reviewed thus: "*The Forgotten Present* does not describe the world. It highlights its marvels like an old child seeing them properly for the first time." (The review section was notorious for its hyperbolic style.)

The Forgotten Present had raised the region's profile by glorifying rural life. This had in turn resulted in increasing numbers of vacationers and increasing numbers of vacation homes and increasing numbers of marketgoers, all of whom felt vaguely nostalgic and therefore greeted every item they recognized from their childhood or vacations with their grandparents like a long-lost friend.

Géraldine Châtelet and Jean Finkielkraut remained resolutely oblivious to each other's presence, however, one always passing when the other had just turned around. It was maddening!

Who knows if their whole lives would have been turned inside out had they looked each other in the eye? Of course not. People are not overly keen on believing in genuine miracles after their thirteenth birthday, let alone in love at first sight.

Regarding the moment when two people who have long been connected first meet

A man and a woman are walking along the same street (or two men, or two women, or a seahorse and a hippopotamus). One of them is a northerner, the other a southerner, and they're on the same pavement. When they have closed to within forty or fifty feet of each other, it begins. A look that catches the other's eye, an exchange that lasts a little longer than usual, perhaps a smile, a reaction, a wordless dialogue. They advance toward each other, and their bodies pass through each other's auras.

They share a silent look.

A shock wave. Being so close together, so unfamiliar and yet so near, reunited and close. And all of a sudden *that* feeling: That's him. That's her.

And yet they keep walking, but because the absurd, magical, unique feeling of having met the one and only other doesn't stop, as the other body continues to feed the shock wave—and they know exactly what that body's embrace feels like, but how?—they look around. Or rather: Only one of them does. The other doesn't because he's thinking that this can't be happening: He's just fallen in love, but with someone totally unsuitable/he isn't so unhappily married/he's just popped out to do some shopping.

What are they supposed to do? Turn on their heels, go back and take this unique hand, walk on to a hotel together, savor each other, celebrate this unsought-for reunion, catch their breath, look at each other, and think, *My God, what if we'd just carried on walking?*

That's not possible, I hear you say. Well, if you still don't believe this is genuinely possible, then there's nothing I can do for you.

There's also that other situation when a loving couple plays that delightful "Do you remember?" game. ("Anyway, I wasn't going to go to the party, but Monique, who was only over at my place because—you won't believe this—someone had run over her toe with a shopping cart the week before! And she'd been in a part of town where I wouldn't normally even get off the bus, but someone had died at her usual baker's and it was closed, but she was desperate for an apple-cinnamon bun. . . . Anyway, Monique told me to go to the party and say hi for her, and so there I was and that's how we met—just imagine if I'd done as I'd intended and gone to bed that evening with a slice of cake, wondering why I was still living on my own.") They list all the things that had to go right for them to meet, and if just one little detail had been wrong (no death at Monique's baker's, or if the guy who ran over her foot had been carrying a basket rather than pushing a cart, and so on and so forth), then they would have walked past each other.

Why? Because arranging all these little details is a full-time job. Fate does its best—or sometimes doesn't, because, after all, it isn't Happiness or even an author.

Oh yes: Love at first sight is nothing other than love at first resighting.

Marie-Jeanne emerged from her bewildered state and embraced Pragmatism. Pragmatism had entered her life at Logic's suggestion, poured a bucket of decisiveness and unthinking gumption over the girl, and then disappeared again before the olive tree could even begin to say, "Um, there's something you should know before you . . . Oh, all right. Too late."

What was a budding young woman with two and a half handfuls of years under her belt and a long plait supposed to do? "Bonjour, madame. Allow me to introduce you to the man whom you've been cooking for and discussing books with in your imagination for about ten years now. Here he is."

Why not, actually? Why make things more complicated than they already were?

She was about to start off after Madame Châtelet when she had second thoughts. There was a risk that the woman wouldn't believe her, however open she otherwise was to outrageous ideas.

She watched them as Madame Châtelet asked for some olives and Jean Finkielkraut selected goat cheese. How easy it would be for them to share an aperitif with their purchases. She sensed that the door in time was creaking and would soon slam shut. Only one or two heartbeats remained. . . .

Her mind raced at the speed of a falling pebble, and then inspiration struck.

"Bonjour, Monsieur Finkielkraut."

"Marie-Jeanne! I hardly recognized you—you look so grown-up. Has your father noticed?"

"Probably not. Perhaps you could tell him sometime?"

They smiled at each other. She had always liked him because he didn't speak to her like she was a child and his butterfly theory had induced her to take a helter-skelter ride through the diverse world of books.

She leaned closer to him. "You reserved a book by Simone Weil?"

"That's right," he said. "Is it available now?"

"No, Madame Châtelet still has it. Should I ask her when she thinks she'll have finished with it?"

"No, no, that would be rude. Um, who is this Madame . . . ?"

Marie-Jeanne pointed her out. Géraldine was standing only a few yards away with her eyes closed, totally absorbed as she sniffed a melon from Carpentras.

"She reads Simone Weil?" Jean asked after a few seconds.

"Not only Weil. All the existentialists, feminists, and also other philosophers, including Kant, Foucault, Nietzsche, Adorno, and Kierkegaard."

"I see."

"She has lots of time," Marie-Jeanne said. "You know, living alone."

"Really?"

"And she can cook all the recipes in Elsa's cookbook from memory."

"I see!"

Then Marie-Jeanne did something she could only hope

would work. She looked Jean Finkielkraut straight in the eye and thought as loudly as she could, *YOU'VE LOVED EACH OTHER FOR YEARS!*

"I see," he said after a while, as if he had been contemplating whether he had just heard something or merely imagined it.

Something incredible.

Something fantastic.

Something impossible.

I could see that a small sun had risen in his heart.

"Forgive me, but I have to, um . . ." he said, his eyes suddenly faraway and silvery blue, like the washed-out blue where the sea meets the sky. He had completely forgotten about Marie-Jeanne and slowly advanced toward Madame Châtelet.

Please let this work, the girl whispered to herself.

Jean's pace slowed even further. Was he going to drop down dead in the final yards?

Come on!

The writer paused just before he reached Madame Châtelet.

I could see that the rising sun was followed by a brewing thunderstorm of worry and fear. The nasty little censor in his head was murmuring: *Oh please, will you look at yourself? And look at her. Obvious, isn't it?*

. . .

Marie-Jeanne felt that if she rolled her eyes any more they would drop out of her head. But then . . . He was moving again! Quickly even, and purposefully.

Quickly and purposefully, Monsieur Finkielkraut walked straight past Madame Châtelet.

Marie-Jeanne was too distraught for thought.

On the deceptive idyll of waiting

Waiting is probably the most amazing promise we can make to ourselves that we will be rewarded for the time we have invested. Waiting for someone. Waiting for inspiration, courage, or the energy to make a decision. Waiting for Christmas, salvation, release, divorce, or death. Waiting for the other person to call back, to break up, to say the right word, to come back. Listening to ourselves as we wait, or trying desperately not to. Trying to keep the present exactly as it is as we wait, so as not to jeopardize the future. Waiting for our turn, in every sense: to get what we want, to be happy, to buy two pounds of new potatoes, to fall in love. And sometimes, even more deceptively, the noble and humble occupation of waiting is not waiting but simple gutlessness.

26

The Night of Wishes

The "night of wishes" was what the old folks called the hours between the twelfth and the thirteenth of August, just after the feast of St. Lawrence, a night when the Perseid meteor shower rained down from the dark firmament of the night.

The storm of shooting stars started after midnight, when children were usually in bed, listening out for the breath of darkness. However, on the night of wishes, people of all ages were allowed to stay up, and the entire population of Nyons did. Everyone in all the valleys between the four mountains was awake, and they were all in the quietest part of their garden, staring in the same direction—upward, with their heads thrown back. The women sat on chairs, the children huddled in the sun-dried grass, and the men loitered in the deepest shadows, as if no one should see the expressions on their faces as they made their silent wishes.

Marie-Jeanne could smell the oleander, bougainvillea, jasmine, rosemary, and sage. She pictured Jean Finkielkraut sitting in his garden on his own, a glass of wine in his hand, counting the different fragrances.

"Moron," she whispered.

She pictured Géraldine Châtelet filling two glasses and yelling at the heavens, *"I've spent a thousand lives wishing for the same man, so stop pouring stars on my head. I don't believe a word of it!"*

She had returned the Simone Weil she had borrowed, but Marie-Jeanne still couldn't bring herself to ride out to Jean's house to lend him the book. He could come and get it himself!

For some reason, she felt personally offended that he had lost heart in the final few yards. What was so hard about saying "Bonjour, madame" or "May I have the pleasure of inviting you to a café? Go right ahead if you fancy a glass of champagne."

My goodness, that's why we read books! They describe such rational methods in detail.

Why were adults so afraid of making mistakes, as if they were only allowed to commit a certain number and one more would see them topple off their horses dead? What was wrong with them?

To distract herself, Marie-Jeanne thought of Vida Lagetto dreaming, eyes wide, as she looked up at the sky. She hoped Vida would make a wish to go out into the world.

How about Madame Colette, the calligraphy expert? Would she wish for a man to write down his name on a piece of paper and give it to her?

She thought of Loulou, who was fast becoming a woman, and little Sylvaine and Madeleine sitting on the laps of their big sisters, Martine and Noëlle. Loulou would be alone and exhausted somewhere in the dark, weeping to herself. Should she wish for what she had long forbidden herself to wish for? That Luca should give her another of those looks she could never explain, which put her in a state of rage, mixed with a much subtler sensation. A feeling she could only understand on the verge of sleep. A quiet, serious, small, and precious sensation.

One short sentence: "I don't wish to be without him." And then the shooting stars began to fall.

Some exploded out of nowhere and their trails faded away slowly and dreamily, others took their time, and it was never clear where the next dazzling green meteor would appear. Blink and you missed an *étoile filante,* born of the starry foam around the constellations of Perseus and Cassiopeia.

Elsa tilted her head back until it was almost resting on Francis's shoulder. Almost. She would have loved to do so, but what if he pulled his shoulder away, gently, almost imperceptibly, and yet still deliberately?

You have each other, Marie-Jeanne thought. *You belong together. Don't waste so much precious time!*

What on earth was wrong with people? What made them so cowardly and fearful? What did they stand to lose, other than time apart?

The sky was already ablaze with hundreds of ephemeral solicitations of the world's wishes. Hundreds and hundreds of answers floated up to them from people's gardens and rooms.

Marie-Jeanne shut her eyes. She listened out, and secret wishes came streaming toward her in untold numbers.

I wish for a different life.

I wish she would look at me as she used to.

I wish I had enough money to buy a Mercedes.

I wish I had a room of my own, or just a bed, or at least five minutes per day when I'm alone. Just five minutes to myself.

I wish we could make love.

I wish I had Luca.

I wish I had Loulou.

I wish you would come back, and even if I could never just be your friend, the way you want me to be, and no more—I can't do it, my feelings for you are too strong, do you hear that? far too strong—then my wish is still that you would come back into my life. I miss you. I trip over your name, the memory of your face, the way you looked at me. Every day.

So much longing in the world. So much tugging of heartstrings.

I send this thought to you on a night when the stars are falling from the sky.

I don't know your face. I don't know your name and I won't tell you mine.

The day we stand face-to-face, the day we touch, we will know we are the ones.

Marie-Jeanne opened her eyes. Hang on, she knew this prayer. It was the start of a letter in one of the books. How could anyone have left something like that in a library book? Was it a message in a bottle? A request to chance and fate to allow this sheet of paper to fulfill its sacred mission and deliver it to its intended recipient?

"Where are you going?" Elsa asked.

Marie-Jeanne mumbled something unintelligible.

"Sorry?"

But the girl had already gone, because she'd realized

what she could do with all the searching southern lights whose aching desires weighed on her heart, their silent cries echoing in her head. She absolutely had to sit down and think about her plan in private. The best thing would be to write it down.

If none of these people dared to take the first step, she needed to adopt radical means to help them, or go mad.

Impatient Marie-Jeanne Claudel's crazy plan

1. Get Loulou to write out her full name on a sheet of handmade paper from Madame Brillant the calligrapher's store (secretly steal the paper) without telling Loulou what it's for (if necessary, invent a white lie).

2. Draft a love letter to Luca on this same piece of paper with some assistance from a long-dead love poet called Rumi. Same procedure in reverse for Luca.

3. Insert the love prayer Madame Châtelet put into words as a bookmark into Jean Finkielkraut's next book.

4. Make up an obscure reason for Monsieur Finkielkraut to take the book directly to Madame Châtelet, resorting to some over-the-top emotional appeal such as "It's a matter of life and death."

5. Ask Francis to kiss Elsa's hands. If he questions it, claim to have read somewhere that it brings luck.

6. Find out to whom Vida Lagetto's southern light leads. Ditto for Madame Brillant's. Hope that she and Napoléonne don't have to ride to Timbuktu and back for this.

7. Save all the wishes. They're permitted tonight, but they'll only come true if people mean them. Isn't that true?

27

Everyone Is Entitled to Be a Fool in Love

Marie-Jeanne had pondered her list long and hard, and as she rode out into the happy, fragrant morning, she had had an unpleasant realization. She needed an accomplice. She wouldn't be able to manage alone.

There was only one possible candidate. Who else, if not a mythology specialist well versed in the world's wonders and legends and ancient lore, with an open mind for the most unprecedented events? So Marie-Jeanne spurred foam-white Napoléonne toward Montjoux.

Madame Montesquieu had spent the night outside under a mosquito net, and when Marie-Jeanne came upon her there she could see that Valérie was smiling in her sleep. Eyes still closed, she said, "Good morning, my dear."

Napoléonne made friends with the wild and beautiful garden in no time. Valérie and Marie-Jeanne sat down in the pleasant coolness of the kitchen, while the sun's heat built up underneath the trees and the cicadas struck up their rhythmical summer song.

The girl told her everything. The sparks, the lights at night, the glowing—and all her crazy plans.

"Hmm," Valérie said. "Yes . . . Yes, that makes total sense. Where did you say I had this southern light?"

"On your lips. It flashes every time you say something clever. If someone touches those spots, I imagine love must feel especially close and, um, intense. Is that right?"

"I never thought anyone would ask me something like that, but yes, it's true. Whenever someone has touched me gently on my lips, even just brushing them with their fingers, best of all here"—she ran a finger over her lower lip—"I felt particularly loved. It meant that person loved looking at me, which was the best reason to open my eyes."

"And you miss him?"

"Him?" Valérie asked softly.

The blush that inflamed the girl's cheeks held its own against the profuse rambling roses in the background. "Oh, I'm sorry."

"Oh, not at all, my dear! I was at least as surprised as you are that I wanted to spend my life with someone who was my best friend and favorite intellectual sparring partner. We liked each other a lot and loved each other a lot too. Of course, love doesn't necessarily mean you have to share a bedroom or rip off all your clothes and underwear every time you're together. Lovers can love each other without ever kissing. That's because the points of love are, you know, not identical to the points of lust."

"That's not likely to please the priest."

"Not likely, no. But queer people like me can have desire without love and love without lust."

"It occurs to me that I really don't have any idea about this, um, *thing*." Marie-Jeanne's mind turned to the *romans à l'eau de rose* with the pirates and unhappily married damsels swooning in their arms, and all the metaphors Elsa weighed carefully in her mouth before letting them out into the world.

"You don't? You have your whole life ahead of you to kiss and be kissed by whoever you like. That's fine *with* love but it's also perfectly fine *without* love. Whatever makes you feel good."

Marie-Jeanne muttered, "I think I'd like to have a pretend coughing fit now to hide my embarrassment. Is that possible?"

"Be my guest. Let yourself go. I'll just keep talking and leave out the more awkward bits. Would that work for you?"

Cue coughing.

"So then, love. Every new love is basically the first love. It's like forgetting everything we've learned and starting from scratch each time. That happens because we haven't a clue about love, which is a good thing."

"We're not meant to understand love?"

Valérie looked dreamily around her house, whose walls seemed to be listening in on their conversation. "That's right. We can *assume* we're in love when we start doing inexplicable and reckless things. You know, I for one shut myself away. I couldn't easily go outside because she was everywhere I turned. And everywhere she was missing. There were holes everywhere—in the village, the countryside, the towns, the mountains, the sky. She was missing from the forests and the stars and the rain and the cafés, even the market. From everything. The only thing I could see was what wasn't there. I found the thought of going back out into a world lacking the person I no longer had unbearable. Death is weaker than love. It doesn't put an end to love. But . . . what do you think you will experience in love in the future that you don't understand now?"

"Nothing, probably. I don't have . . . a southern light. I'll never see the world with gaps in it."

Valérie took Marie-Jeanne's hands in hers. The girl's fingers resting in the older woman's well-worn, wrinkly, cupped hands were small and smooth.

"And what makes you think that? Why were you given such an ability to love, and why should you be denied your own?"

"I don't know," Marie-Jeanne whispered. "Can you live alone without loving someone?"

"Of course you can," Valérie said quickly.

"You are touching up the facts."

"You're capable of love," Valérie remarked gently. "That's clear from the fact that you are trying to soothe the hearts of those who are dear to you. Why else, if I may point out, would you have such silly ideas about shoehorning them together rather than leaving them to overcome their inhibitions?"

"I can't just stand by and do nothing!"

"True," Valérie said. "That should never be an option for a woman."

The previous night Marie-Jeanne had assumed that she'd understood the crux of the matter and could get going, but now she realized that she might as well have taken a sock, stuffed it with a few hard apples, tied a knot in it, and banged herself over the head with it.

With a sigh she said, "So at the end of a fairy tale it should now say, 'And they lived happily ever after until love started causing trouble.' I get the feeling that all these couples have already caused far too much trouble."

Valérie laughed out loud. "That's true. But you know what, Marie-Jeanne? Love is a rose and—"

"My father says that love is a house and every room needs to be inhabited."

"Your father is a clever man. To my mind the rose epitomizes love. You see, lots of people think love has to be a scented flower without thorns, but that is to misunderstand the nature of love."

"I think Loulou sees the rose as being more like a cactus."

Valérie clasped the girl's hands more tightly. "Which is why you want to save her. I know you do. But imagine if you got a letter like that from someone who is a rose to you—beautiful and painful at the same time. Then one day you discover that the person you thought was baring his soul to you has completely different handwriting. You have a nagging doubt: Would he ever have written to me of his own accord? You shouldn't underestimate how agonizing it is to live with that doubt. You have to give people space."

"But it's plain to see! They are made for each other like . . . like, I don't know, waffles and caramel ice cream. It's so stupid. They're the stupid ones, not me."

"Let people be fools in love! Sometimes people lie to themselves about love. Loving and not noticing, or not believing they're in love. Constantly trying to convince themselves that it's only desire, it's mere force of habit, it's only attraction or friendship. Yet in the end the habit lasts a lifetime. That too is love, and some people only notice at the very end. In essence, humans are always susceptible to the misfortune of being only what they are." Satisfied with herself, Valérie reached for her bowl of café au lait. "That's how I see it anyway. Do you have any more questions?"

"I'm worried that a revolution has just broken out in my head," Marie-Jeanne replied.

"Hmm, that isn't the worst outcome. Have you contemplated lifting the visor of your helmet and speaking out? As you've done to me. It would spare you some tricky situations, like having to break into Colette Brillant's house, falsify documents, and lie to your friend."

"That would be a pretty crazy step to take, so no, not really. Why would they believe me? Should I drop it then? Just stand by and watch?"

"Would you be happy doing that?"

"Not really."

Marie-Jeanne thought things through. If she could get Jean to return the book with Géraldine's letter inside and sit down on the terrace next to the white cat, then . . . His heart would skip and pound, his brain would freeze, and there would be no guarantee that he'd be able to get his exquisite phrases in order if Madame Châtelet was around. She couldn't carry him into the lady's bed or spell out to him what he ought to say, the right words. *Hold on a second. Words.*

Words, words, words. How did it go? Books are the last great alchemy of our age. They create, transform, and vanquish time, death, and fear. They create invisible realities. They are the silent doors through which we walk to find ourselves.

Marie-Jeanne's eyes fell on the saddlebags with the books inside them. She had put them next to the outdoor table so Napoléonne would be slightly less squeezed around her middle.

Books, those discreet accomplices. Place a book between two people and see what happens between them. Let a little light shine into their hearts and give them a chance to see better.

It went *bing!* inside Marie-Jeanne, and before it could do so a second time—*bing-bing!*—she blurted out, "You wouldn't be interested in hosting a literary salon with accompanying aperitifs, would you, Madame Montesquieu? Maybe up at Vida's hotel, La Dolce Vita, with invitations written in Madame Colette's best calligraphy? We could suggest that Monsieur Finkielkraut give a little talk about writing and discuss the books people have read, handwriting, and life in general. We would invite a few handpicked guests, you know who, and—"

"You little devil, you," Valérie whispered. "If they ever find out that we're trying to matchmake, they'll never speak to us again." She flashed the girl a youthful and mischievous smile. "I'm in! What should we call the salon? The Lonely Hearts' Book Club?"

"I'd be in favor of a slightly more subtle name," Marie-Jeanne suggested.

28

Some Short Character Descriptions

Loulou Raspail could now embroider, make lace, juggle, and recite poetry; had started learning Italian; and was doing the early shift in the bakery. All to drive these damn thoughts of Luca out of her mind, but there was no hope of that.

Luca had settled on reading, swimming, and working at the olive press. As a result, he was in a terrible mood, overworked and totally lost. He slept badly, had wild dreams, and clung even more to Béatrice, as Loulou did to André. Okay, it was boring, but wasn't boredom the antechamber to inner peace?

They were shells of their former selves, ruins of a young love that was now visiting very adult torments on them. So they were extraordinarily grateful to receive invitations to the opening session of the literary salon organized by the Philis Mobile Library—Literary Loans and Orders. They felt extremely grown-up.

The invitations were by name only—no plus-ones—and it was not called a literary salon but Littéramour.

"Ah, a blend of literature and love. It doesn't get more subtle than that," Valérie remarked politely.

"It's only not subtle if you know what the intention is."

Madame Colette Brillant, who had been left in the dark about the plan, had designed the invitation and was delighted, surprised, and not a little excited when she found the card in her letterbox down in the village a few days later. A literary salon—how charming! She realized, as she stood helplessly in front of her meager wardrobe and wondered what on earth to wear, that she hadn't been down from her mountainside for as long as she could remember.

The other invitees were Jean Finkielkraut, the famous local writer (this point had now finally been acknowledged, much to his satisfaction); the tango-dancing solicitor Géraldine Châtelet; Elsa Malbec; Francis Meurienne; their host, Vida Lagetto; the mobile librarian and occasional mythology expert Valérie Montesquieu; Luca and Loulou; the bookseller Monsieur Mussigmann (as a decoy); and—to Valérie and Marie-Jeanne's great pride and significant concern—the two presumed matches for Vida's and Colette's southern lights.

Would these last two come? Or would one of them disappear off to the coast and the other ignore an opportunity a second time?

The two accomplices had discovered the identities of these two individuals by crisscrossing the surrounding countryside in Louis the Fourth from dusk to dawn for weeks in pursuit of the threads the two ladies sent out. Eventually they had tracked them down.

They had told Elsa and Francis that Valérie was teaching Marie-Jeanne astronomy. This was in fact not entirely untrue because the older woman recounted every love and horror story she knew. As they pursued the southern lights, the girl soaked up the latest gossip from Roman, Greek, Native American, and Mayan myths, as well as a few saucy anecdotes regarding Indian, Japanese, and Chinese astronomy and also some long-lost legends.

Following Vida's southern light had proved a challenge. That was because Vida went to bed late and got up early, devoting a huge chunk of her waking life to running the hotel. As a result, her southern light often rolled itself into a tight ball while it was still dark. One day, however, she had slept in. Her light had been visible to Marie-Jeanne well into the morning and she had been able to guide Valérie up mountain roads and across viaducts.

It led them to one of the hotel's regular patrons, by the name of Édouard Théophile Jacques Léopold de la Tour, who preferred to be known as Édou and took offense if he was referred to by his lengthy aristocratic moniker. All the latter signified, in Édou's opinion, was that he had been preceded by a series of people whose deepest desire had been to ruin their innocent newborn successors' fun by lumbering them with a lot of gibberish.

Édou in three words: shy, magnanimous, observant. It's hardly worth mentioning that he only stayed at Vida's hotel for one reason, and it had nothing to do with the quality and variety of her breakfast buffet. He lived in one of those forgotten *manoirs,* which only his presence prevented from crumbling into dust. Unbeknownst to her, Vida had left an indelible imprint on his life. He owned clothes that he had bought simply so he could wear them to her establishment.

Glasses too. His constant question to himself was: Will she like this? He had a useless feeling of being vain, was obsessed with pleasing her, and failed to recognize a passion that was kindled neither by glasses nor by the cut of his shirt (seriously).

People could be attracted by a tiny stain on a dress or jacket, though. A microscopic imperfection.

He admired Vida for following her own personal path in life. He loved the way she treated people. He respected her for ignoring him.

Édou's beautiful, slender fingers played with the invitation. He really did have remarkably beautiful hands that radiated serenity and wisdom.

"Forgive me for asking, mesdames, but is it correct that Madame Lagetto did not send this invitation herself?"

"That is unfortunately correct," Valérie replied.

"And what makes you think that I would be, um, welcome there?"

"*You* do," Marie-Jeanne said. "You know you would be welcome there." She looked him in the eye and repeated the words she had telepathically addressed to Jean Finkielkraut on the market square in Nyons: *BECAUSE YOU LOVE VIDA, AND SHE LOVES YOU.*

Even if she isn't fully aware of that yet, she added to herself.

Vida did indeed feel a slight irritation, but she barred herself *strictement* from thinking about this in any detail. She did wonder why he was always there, but, well, that's what regular guests do. She had no reason to imagine that it was personal.

Édouard Théophile Jacques Léopold de la Tour was a man who decided to face up to the wonders of life with a courage that so many others lacked. He gazed into Marie-Jeanne's eyes for a long time.

"Did you know," he began, and the girl's heart started to crackle with life (he spoke to her with a respect that was blind to the age of the person he was addressing), "that I drive to the coast when I don't know what to do next? The sea is so rich and full. It never hesitates. Maybe we should all go to the seaside more often to lose ourselves so that we can then find ourselves again. I shall drive to the coast and there I shall find the man I need to be in order to spend this evening with you and with Madame Lagetto. It must not be the cowardly side of me, if you see what I mean."

The way his voice caressed Vida's surname.

"Perfect. Then we shall expect this other gentleman around seven," Valérie had answered.

Love is sometimes a wound that a man carries around silently inside him. He sees one specific woman and to him she is a wonder, whereas to others she is invisible. The skill lies in approaching the wonder in spite of the wound.

The search for Colette the calligrapher's southern light had been even more laborious. It led south to the sea. To a chef. His name was Pierre Moissonnier and he owned a restaurant in Sanary-sur-Mer. And so it was that Marie-Jeanne got her first sighting of the sea in her thirteenth year of life, and her only regret was that Napoléonne couldn't stroll along the quayside with her. How silken the colors were, how sparkling the water!

Valérie and Marie-Jeanne waited on the beach, dipping their feet in the water, until Pierre had served all his lunchtime diners and they could make their case to him—an invitation to a literary salon in Nyons, a three-hour drive from Sanary.

"I'm deeply honored, mesdames, but, if I may, what makes you think that I in particular might be tempted?"

"It's highly possible that you'll meet the love of your life there."

"Oh really? In that case, the answer's yes."

Actually, I made that last bit up.

Marie-Jeanne had noticed Pierre's menus and so she answered his question by placing the elegant literary salon invitation, penned by Madame Colette, on a table.

The chef sat down cautiously.

"I know this penmanship," he said after a while.

"Do you know the penwoman too?"

He shook his head.

"This would be a very convenient opportunity to meet her."

That's right. Colette Brillant had once designed the menus for Pierre's restaurant, albeit without ever tasting the dishes she had so stylishly translated into vibrant, mouthwatering letters and without ever meeting the chef who had commissioned her to write their names. Her hands had savored them, though. She had dreamed her way into the question of who might have the talent to concoct such delicacies with such finesse.

When her calligraphy samples arrived, Pierre had studied them at length and felt an odd recurring pang in his chest because rarely had he seen anything so beautiful. This handwriting transcended everything. It was as if the written words were detached from all his duties and responsibilities and frustrations. They shone with a promise of freedom and joy.

And yet he had never dared to investigate whose hand was responsible for this handwriting. First, he had had more than enough on his plate; second, he didn't want to seem intrusive; and third, it was so long ago. And thus ten years had passed.

"Ten?!"

"Yes. And then, you know, I thought that it was maybe a tiny little bit late now."

"That's incredible. You seem a considered man," Valérie said as politely as ever, although she felt a very unladylike urge to throttle him. "You can consider the invitation too, but maybe reach a decision a little more quickly this time?"

Pierre's eyes had glazed over at the sight of Colette's handwriting after all these years. He had nice eyes, green with a dense wreath of lashes seldom observed in men, and he was warmhearted too. And he could cook. What could possibly go wrong? Okay, he didn't read very much. Or rather, not at all. He did promise to take a closer look at one book at least, though, so Valérie and Marie-Jeanne left him Jules Verne's *Journey to the Center of the Earth*.

Everything is connected to everything.

"Are they going to come?" Marie-Jeanne asked as Louis the Fourth gamely negotiated the slopes north of Marseille, that great, bone-white city.

"I don't know, my darling. Each new day lays itself at your feet like a promise. That's all life can do."

29

The Littéramour Book Club

"They've actually come," Valérie whispered.

The guests were standing around a little awkwardly after having greeted one another with the customary *bise* on each cheek. They were clutching their champagne flutes a little too tightly and sipping from them a little too quickly.

Édou had calmly and unhesitatingly made himself useful by topping up everyone's glasses. Vida wended her way through the crowd, offering little canapés such as slices of toast spread with delicious olive and tomato tapenade, and fried sardines with her homemade lemon mayonnaise—a legend in the making. All the while, the chef from Sanary-sur-Mer was devouring Colette Brillant with eyes as large and silent as those of a Mediterranean sprat. His dog-eared copy of Jules Verne's novel lay before him on a side table as he abruptly started talking to Vida about different ways of preparing mayonnaise.

At the same time, Colette was chatting rather too enthusiastically to Jean Finkielkraut for Marie-Jeanne's liking, and Géraldine Châtelet was involved in a fierce discussion with Elsa Malbec over the best way to protect books from grease stains. Luca and Loulou were busy ignoring each other. Francis was examining his fingernails.

All in all, it seemed a perilous exercise to cater to the happiness of all these fine people.

Marie-Jeanne lit a few candles and turned off the ceiling lights. The guests' faces immediately looked prettier and softer.

Monsieur Mussigmann came rushing in with a big plastic tub full of new titles and casually began to talk to those standing nearest to him. His anecdotes about authors' lives soon relaxed the tension and spread laughter through the room.

"You know, Charles Dickens left his wife and ten children for a young actress."

"Oh, you beastly man! You're ruining *A Christmas Carol* for me."

"I didn't mean to do that, Madame Brillant. But did you know that Freud couldn't stand tartare sauce or that Bram Stoker got food poisoning from crab salad before he sat down to write *Dracula*? The incalculable effects of food on a sensitive soul . . ."

"*Dracula?*" Francis inquired quietly.

"Currently out on loan," Elsa whispered back. "Lots of metaphors."

"Agatha Christie, on the other hand, comes up with her murder stories in the bath. She does have running hot water, mind you."

"I'm so envious," Géraldine sighed.

"Right. And the new Simenon has just arrived. Georges Simenon wears the same shirt while he's writing a new detective novel. For weeks and weeks, so that his flow is not interrupted. Schiller, however, would leave apples in his desk drawer to rot so that the smell would put him in the mood. Aha, but Joseph Roth—"

"I'm not sure I really care to imagine all of this," Vida said. "Would you like a canapé, Monsieur Mussigmann?"

"So," Valérie whispered to Marie-Jeanne, "what can you see?"

"Sparking, glowing, humming, threading, knotting, and, more than anything, that none of it is very, um, orderly. It's all a bit of a mess. Threads that don't belong together are getting tangled up. It's as if they're sizing one another up or testing one another out. I'm wondering . . ."

"Go on."

"I'm wondering if things aren't going to turn out quite differently."

"How do you mean?"

"Maybe it's like this. Every person is born with love and goes out into the world with that love. But it isn't love that decides whom we love—it's us."

"That's an intriguing alternative perspective."

"Would that be bad?"

"Maybe for some. All of us long for it to be fate. I don't really know, but I like your theory that we come into the world with love and we can choose whom we love. As long as we don't fall in love with the wrong person, that is."

"What do you mean?"

A cough close by. "Shouldn't we start our literary debate," Madame Châtelet asked, "before Monsieur Mussigmann treats us to more intimate facts about the great minds?"

"Speaking of great minds, when Goethe went to the, um, bathroom—"

"Of course we should, my dear!" Valérie replied hurriedly. With her delicate lace-edged parasol in her hand, she walked daintily over to an armchair piled high with firm cushions.

Marie-Jeanne didn't really listen to the mythology expert–cum–librarian's greeting—it was about affinities, literary families, and the fact that there were no right or wrong opinions when it came to discussing books—because her mind was still wrestling with the following puzzle: *We can choose whom we love, as long as we don't love the wrong person.*

The evening was organized around three books: *A Certain Smile* by Françoise Sagan, *Journey to the Center of the Earth* by Jules Verne, and *No Exit* by Jean-Paul Sartre. It was all there—love, adventure, philosophy. A different dish was served to accompany each book, and there was no skimping on alcoholic conversational aids either.

Géraldine and Jean immediately got into a rumpus over the starter: trout carpaccio with Sartre.

"Sartre may have written that hell is other people, but actually every hell begins inside us, in our dishonesty toward ourselves, and—"

"May I interrupt you, madame, because—"

"No, you may not, monsieur. I cannot stand being interrupted."

"Wine, anyone?" Vida asked.

"Let me give you a hand," Édou said very quietly and very tenderly. "And I would suggest that you take a seat here."

"But, monsieur. You are my guest and—"

"Would you be offended if *I* were to serve *you*?"

"Oh, on reflection, I don't think so," said Vida, sliding into an armchair. She realized that she'd never acted like a guest in her own hotel before. It was very pleasant indeed.

"What I find strange about the whole thing is that Lidenbrock doesn't think it's at all hellish there," the chef contributed.

"Didn't Jules Verne do a dive as a guinea pig first?" the solicitor said sternly.

"Don't your ears hurt in the deep sea?" Colette tossed into the conversation. She didn't much appreciate Madame Châtelet giving the chef a hard time. "Why does no one ever mention ear pains, not even Dante?"

"Uhum," the chef said gallantly in an attempt to cover up his total ignorance about Dante. He was glad that his question hadn't been ignored, though.

"I'd like some wine," Francis said.

Édou inclined the bottle.

"No, he wouldn't," Elsa said.

He served her first and then Francis before adding in a low voice, "You two should clink glasses. These ones make such a lovely sound."

Elsa blushed slightly but followed his advice. The glasses chimed, and she gazed into her husband's eyes. A strange tingle went through her body. When had she last looked him in the eye or at his nice mouth?

"The insincerity of assimilating rather than making the most of freedom . . ." Géraldine really did not like being interrupted and had immediately resumed her commentary on Sartre.

"So?" Loulou hissed to poor Luca. "What's boring Béatrice up to tonight?"

". . . or escaping conventions, whatever the consequences."

"Probably the same as your annoying André."

An intermittent sparkle, but they were just getting warmed up.

"Ha! But madame surely cannot demand that people exclude themselves from the community simply to preserve their sincerity. That degree of individuality goes against human nature."

"You're putting words into my mouth, Monsieur Finkielkraut."

"Now, the main course is—"

"You didn't even need to say it, madame; you were thinking it. When I asked Sartre himself, in person—"

"Goodness, I see that monsieur hobnobs with the high and mighty."

"Were you being sarcastic, madame?"

"What do *you* think? Do you even know the difference between sarcasm and irony, monsieur?" Géraldine's eyebrows twitched upward and her lips flickered into a smile Marie-Jeanne had never seen before. It wasn't a mocking smile. She was amused. Entertained, even.

Marie-Jeanne was reminded of Luca and Loulou's spats, although Madame Châtelet and Monsieur Finkielkraut were facing off with much sharper weapons than pulling a girl's hair or stuffing beetles down a boy's back.

"I am quite capable of detecting sarcasm when I encounter it, Madame Châtelet, but yours is undeniably the finest example of hubris in my collection so far."

"I know you don't mean that, Monsieur Finkielkraut, and so I shall choose to take it as a compliment."

The look Géraldine gave the author was somewhere between a stiletto knife in the ribs and the proud come-hither of a tango dancer. All of a sudden, his eyes took on their silvery-blue sheen again.

"I would like some more wine," Colette said.

As Édou filled her glass, Vida felt fantastically relaxed. She was paying only vague attention to the dispute between the philosophical big beasts behind her because virtually all her attention was focused on her regular hotel guest. She realized that she'd never studied him properly before. She had always been too busy. His movements were wonderfully fluid. Clear and decisive, as if he had a fine-tuned inner compass for everything.

Something eased off inside her. It might have been fear.

"You wrote my cards," Pierre suddenly blurted out to Colette.

"Your cards? I . . ."

"Menu cards. I'm, um, you know, from the restaurant La Mirabelle."

The penny slowly dropped inside Colette's head.

"Has anyone noticed that Luc and the first-person narrator in Sagan's novel are also in hell because they are *not* insincere?"

"No."

"Yes they are!"

"Is it already time for dessert?"

"What do you think? Going quite well, isn't it?" Valérie whispered to her young partner.

Marie-Jeanne was not so sure. If you ignored the fact that Loulou and Luca were spitting more and more venom at each other and that Géraldine and Jean were grinning wildly and likely to throttle each other at any moment, everyone else did at least seem capable of sharing the same air. Actually, everything was going fine.

. . .

It was at that moment that I decided not to leave the girl alone with the burden of managing these people's fates. It was presumptuous and it wasn't my job, but I did it all the same: I became Marie-Jeanne's accomplice.

30

Your Name in My Hand

Monsieur Mussigmann told Francis and Elsa more of his shaggy-dog stories—"Oh yes, I swear that Oscar Wilde used to walk a lobster on a leash through the streets of London"—while Luca and Loulou glared at each other in silence, their hearts fit to burst. Important things are so often left unsaid during important conversations, and all the words that were lining up to be stammered out slowly faded into oblivion.

The food was delicious, the wine loosened people's tongues—well, the adults' tongues, anyway; Luca and Loulou had to make do with a shot of black currant liqueur in a glass of water—and at some point Valérie gave up trying to direct the conversation. First Sartre, then Verne, and finally Sagan? Who cared! That had never been the objective anyway. The goal had been to lock a few people in a room together and let candlelight, the alchemy of books, and flavorsome alcohol work their magic.

All that was needed now was for their hearts to grow wings.

. . .

I knew how they grew. Every person presumably has their personal way of communicating. People dance to convey what they cannot express in words. People caress and cuddle and let their bodies say what their mouths won't let them. There ought to be trysts where people can do the things they love without misunderstandings.

Pierre Moissonnier, for example, expressed himself through the dishes he cooked. The way he handled a lemon sole or a red mullet, the way he peeled the leaves from a cabbage and plucked sprigs from bunches of herbs, were different ways of saying: *I respect living creatures and plants and I am full of respect for those who appreciate how nature showers us with gifts for being on this incredible earth.* Pierre was a grateful man. He was thankful for life.

This was precisely what Colette detected, as love for this oddly familiar stranger blossomed inside her. She was similar in character. When she truly opened up to the outside world, it was not through words, even though she put these into calligraphic form. Her breathing, her bearing, her concentration, her care, her playfulness, and her sense of right and wrong were embodied in the relationships between the individual letters, the font she chose, and the thoughts she encapsulated in each word.

Pierre could tell this, albeit without consciously registering it. All he noticed was a repeated rising-and-falling sensation in his tummy and a sudden light feeling in his chest.

He thought of the long drive home the next day and how much time would pass before he saw this woman again. He didn't want to blow another ten years. If only he weren't so shy. He could hardly utter a word.

. . .

I placed my fingers on his lips. On the spot where his southern light was pulsating.

When Colette got up to go and wash her hands, Pierre followed her out into the dimly lit corridor and waited by the telephone table.

"Could I have your phone number?" the chef asked when she returned. "And would you also write down your name? I may seem a little crazy, madame, but I can assure you I'm not. Or maybe I am, but in a good way. It's just that . . . I'd like to see you write something. You created the most beautiful menus in the world for me, and I've been cooking the same dishes ever since, just to keep the menus. I can't believe that such beautiful handwriting exists. And . . . well . . . it's yours."

"You're still cooking the same dishes, all because you like my handwriting?"

" 'Like' is something of an understatement."

Colette's mind was a blizzard of different thoughts. She could say something casual like: "It'd be no trouble to set that right. Send me a handful of new recipes and I'll write them out." Or: "You've surely heard that it's possible to print and photocopy menus nowadays?"

I stepped up beside her. Scanned her heart, gauged her morale, saw her smile.

No, she didn't need my help. The echo within her was so powerful, her memory of the dishes so intense, that even ten summers later, it still haunted her.

. . .

"Do you realize what you're asking of me, Pierre?"

"Yes," he said, but perhaps he was lying a little because he didn't know what Colette Brillant knew: If she gave him a piece of paper with her name on it, she would be his for as long as that note existed. However, he said yes because he felt it was what her question required. He interpreted her question as: "So can I trust that you want everything from me and will give me everything?"

That was the message that entered his heart.

Naturally, Colette's delightful handbag contained everything a woman of letters could possibly need to react to all eventualities with consummate elegance. She took out a fountain pen. It was dark green. She peeled off a sheet of handmade paper from her leather-bound sketchbook as delicately as if she were defusing a bomb. Then she looked the chef in his beautiful green eyes.

"Will you love me?" she asked. No, that's not what she asked. What she actually said was: "So you want my name?" but she meant the former.

She was totally calm and cool and clear in spite of the inner trembling that befell her the longer she stared into the chef's eyes. She wasn't scared of making a mistake now. She wasn't afraid of words now.

"I've already loved you for so long," Pierre wanted to say, "and I will keep on loving you more and more. I shall love you with the constancy with which the waves flood the shore before retreating again. I shall love you with the constancy with which the pole star shines. I shall love you like my child, my sister, my lover, and my friend, like my wife, my accomplice, and my bed. Yes, my bed. Up until now it has been my only home, but I shall love you because you are my home, you are my house. You are the point where everything begins and everything ends."

But instead Pierre simply said, "Yes." A yes that contained the world.

They would have enough time for him to tell her all of those things, over and over again. He would tell her without words, but for her sake he would even learn words. Every word there was.

"Then I would request that you do the same, Monsieur Moissonnier. Give me your name and your phone number. Give me everything about you."

They sat down. She breathed in and out again. Freedom. And then Colette Brillant wrote out her full name on a piece of paper. That was all; the phone number wasn't necessary. She pressed it into the man's hand and she was his.

And he did the same and he was earnest and calm as he did it.

Their exchange of names was a solemn affair, exclusively for the two of them. At a polished wooden table in the quietly lit corridor of a hotel, they promised themselves to each other.

Another person's ambivalence isn't normally laid bare. Jean couldn't see that Madame Châtelet would have loved to beat him with her bare hands to force him away from her, away from her island of loneliness, on which he had suddenly washed up.

There was a silent rage smoldering inside her, a desire to

face him down and even lightly wound him, and at the same time to wrap her arms around her soul. *What's happening to me?* she thought.

He didn't resemble the vague image of a man that she had conjured up for herself over all the lonely years as they ate and danced the tango and clinked glasses as an imaginary couple. This entirely real man sitting here was not elegant and kind. He was sincere, candid, courageous, humane, virile, sensitive, and generous. He loved arguing, and she hadn't realized how electrifying she found it. How sensual.

She imagined what this mouth and this mind might have the audacity to do. What he might dare to do with her and how they might end this row. This delicious, salty row.

Striking back at Jean helped Géraldine breathe more freely. At long last she could fill her lungs. His confrontational attitude allowed her to take a deep breath and show off her intellect and her pugnacity, and he didn't give an inch.

That was exactly what she feared: fulfilling her own great potential in his presence. And that he wouldn't flinch.

The spotlight into which she stepped while facing this man was so dazzling that she made a severe miscalculation. She got to her feet and fled to the bathroom, where she splashed cooling water on her face and drank a cupped handful to calm the fire and breath and electricity inside her.

She caught sight of Colette Brillant next to her in front of the mirror.

"We have lived for far too long to take a backward step now," the calligrapher said to the solicitor. "It would be a betrayal of life. We've no more time to lose, my dear."

But I don't want to cry again, Madame Châtelet thought to herself. *I'm scared of losing this man after being so happy. But I want to speak to this man, go into battle against him, into that combat zone where words come closer than bodies could be, and where among the stabs and the blows and the slaps lurks the knowledge that he feels the same. If we could we would sink our teeth into each other's flesh, hard at first and then softly, until our bites were nothing but breath and tenderness.*

How was she to save herself? How could this be happening to her in the middle of a completely ordinary day?

Géraldine walked out across the wide terrace to consider whether it might not be better just to drive home. Why not? Her Citroën DS promised a swift and stylish exit.

She really was about to leave when I stepped between her and her car. The more two people love each other, the more restlessly they flee and the more urgently they will seek out each other's company again.

Back inside, on that abnormally cool summer's night in Provence, the author summoned up all his unused courage and asked Géraldine directly, furiously, passionately, and unusually inquisitively where she had been all this time.

She knew he didn't mean the previous five minutes but all these years.

"Amazing as it may sound, I was waiting for you at home," she said.

31

The Night of Love

"Come," Francis said to Elsa. "Come with me, my little *garriguette*. Now that everyone's gone, I'll show you the stars."

I thought, *No, Francis, you're going to do something else first*. And so I whispered it to him.

He reached tentatively and gently for her hand, which was resting, clenched as always, beside her dessert plate. He raised her fist to his cheek, whereupon it opened of its own accord, and he ran her fingers lightly over his skin as he closed his eyes. Opening them again, he looked deep into his wife's eyes, bent forward, and kissed her fingers. He lifted them to his face again, and his five o'clock shadow was soft and feathery on her skin.

"Oh, Francis," she said. Or rather, her eyes widened in response to his touch.

"Come on," he said.

They walked across one of the roof terraces hand in hand, within touching distance of the sky, and Francis took Elsa in his arms and held her tight. The fact that they couldn't see each other in the darkness made everything much easier.

"Did you know how beautiful I think you are?" he whispered.

"No. But did you know what a stupid woman I am?"

"No, because you're not."

"I am. I've always had this stupid fear of losing you."

"But that's never going to happen," Francis said. "Didn't you know that? It's never going to happen."

He clasped her hands again and all of a sudden—he didn't know why—it was as if he were seeing them properly for the first time. She had extraordinary hands. Magical hands, for she held his whole life in them.

"You are my wife," he said, "and I am your husband." Kissing her hands again, he added, "And I love you."

"I love you too, Francis," Elsa whispered almost inaudibly, as if she'd found only one last minuscule pocket of air at the very back of her throat. But she had said it. Finally, she had said it!

She began to weep because she no longer needed to fear that she might die without telling him. As her fear of death suddenly vanished, a lust for life came sweeping in with such force that she embraced her husband in tears, cupped his face in her hands, and kissed him as she had long dreamed of kissing him. With the energy of a passionate woman without fear.

She wanted to gaze at him and smile and lose herself in his reciprocations. She wanted all of him, and she grabbed his hands and lifted them to her face. They held each other and stared into each other's eyes. Never before had they kissed this way—silently, attentively—and yet it came so naturally.

They knew each other so well, their lives long intertwined, and now Elsa realized what the saying "Loving is a full-time occupation" meant. This was an aspect of that occupation she particularly enjoyed.

Being a woman of indomitable spirit, Elsa led Francis into one of the empty hotel rooms. There, completely unmetaphorically, they engaged in an activity she no longer wanted only to read about in books. She had a lot of time to make up. The best thing, though, was that the catching up had only just begun.

She let out a joyous laugh.

Meanwhile, Vida put down the empty silver trays and leaned against the large, clear stainless-steel work surface in the middle of the kitchen.

"Why have you been coming here for years, even though you live only twenty minutes away?" she asked without turning to look at Édou, who was tidying up in his beautifully calm and composed manner. "You sleep here, you eat here, you say good night to me, you say good morning to me, but other than that you don't say a word. You look at me when I'm not looking, and I look at you when you're not looking. I noticed today for the first time that I feel cold when you're not looking at me. Who are you, Édouard, and why did you come here this evening?"

Neither of them said anything until she let out a deep sigh.

"I'd like to look you in the eye while I answer that, Vida."

"Oh." She turned around.

"I was invited by Marie-Jeanne Claudel and Valérie Montesquieu. Afterward I drove to the seaside and I asked myself why they'd invited me, but that was the wrong question."

"The wrong question?"

"Yes. The right question is: Who am I, this man who loves you, Vida? Am I a man who dares to tell you that, or, better still, show you? Above all, though, am I a man who will still be there if you kick me out? Because that man would be very different from the man who has been coming here for years, sleeping and eating here and saying good morning but nothing more. I prefer that man to the man who's scared of failure, the one who has waited too long for the right moment, the right words or something. Maybe for the certainty that he wouldn't miss his step and fall. There by the sea I wanted to find a man with no fear of falling. I wanted to find a man with the courage to take a leap, and I wanted that new man to stay."

"That's good, because I want him to stay too," she said, putting her hand over her mouth in surprise at her own words.

I slipped out through the swing doors at the back of the kitchen. It had all been there inside Vida; she had simply misplaced it. I had pried open a tiny, jammed drawer, and inside it was Vida's daring, reckless soul.

Édou nodded and approached her. Vida tilted her head slightly to one side and swept back her hair, gathered it in both hands, and closed her eyes.

He came closer, as close as he could get, and gave her a gentle, warm, playful kiss on the side of her neck, where her nape curved down to her shoulders, innocent and bare. On the exact spot where she glowed. Not that he could see it, though in a sense he could. Vida smiled.

Afterward they cleared up the kitchen together and carried the cheese boards out into the salon. Only Marie-Jeanne and Valérie were still there, so they handed them the cheese and disappeared back into the kitchen.

They had so much to talk about and so much that didn't need saying while they gazed into each other's eyes. They had so much ahead of them. Questions such as: What were you like as a child? What do you dream about?

Kiss me again.

It was a moment of calm, brimming with trust and free of fear. As if they had known each other for decades.

This propitious night had wrapped its mantle around Loulou and Luca too. It enveloped everything in its scent, and the night birds called down from the mountainsides. The two of them longed to embrace; they wanted to shake and hold each other, they wanted to fight because the other had stayed away for so long. They wanted all of this—and they did nothing.

They walked silently down to the swimming pool a long way below the hotel, took off their shoes, sat down on the edge, and dangled their feet in the water. The stars rippled and their feet came close, but not close enough to touch. After a while, the strained sensation of having to say or do something ebbed out of them. They had only to sit there. They didn't need to explain themselves.

Luca ran his hand over Loulou's hair. She shut her eyes, and they lay back in the warm grass as their feet played in the water and made the stars dance. Their hands came together. Their fingers intertwined. They were united.

He propped himself up on his elbow and bent over her. Caressing fingers, stroking hands. And still no words.

What a night of love. A night when everyone came under its loving protection.

32

The Most Beautiful Thing About Love Is the Final Yard

The morning after the night of love, Loulou woke up as herself again. It was only then that she realized she'd tried to become someone else. To her dismay it had worked so well that she had completely fooled herself.

Her first thought was that she would have to tell André she didn't love him. Her second was that Luca hadn't kissed her.

He really didn't kiss me. He merely stroked my hair from time to time, my face, my eyebrows, and my lips—which were still burning from not being kissed! We didn't speak, we didn't act, and we didn't resolve anything. Nothing at all. And yet I'm myself again.

To lie in the beating heart of time, to see the night and the stars fade away until only his eyes remained and to stare up into his eyes as they gazed continually into her own. There it was, the single bright point to which the whole world was attached and around which it revolved. There it was, between them, radiating calm but also the origin of motion. Here she was herself.

This sensation was so strong that it was as if Loulou were still lounging beside the pool of Vida's hotel with that rising-

and-falling feeling in her tummy, touching and stroking and watching her companion's face above her. It felt as if it had been going on for a lifetime.

It hadn't been an easy life. Oh no. She had been furious so many times, and rightly so. How sweet her rage had tasted when she realized that she could drive the young man into a fury. How she'd enjoyed getting under his skin.

Marie-Jeanne was right. That was her first clear thought.

It was visible if you looked hard enough, but only with your own eyes and with your whole self. Not with the alter ego that is terrified of the real self and in a hurry to squash it into a handy small box or frame it in a way that's bearable for you and others.

It is this moody real self, gratified by raging, rows, and reconciliation, and anything but reasonable, kind, and nice, that can see the glowing.

The day after the salon, Colette packed up her inks and her writing and drawing utensils, climbed into her car, and drove farther and farther south to Sanary-sur-Mer. Once there, she strolled along the narrow streets between the fishing village's pastel-colored façades and surrendered to the smells and sounds of the southern seaside issuing from the bistros, restaurants, and cafés.

She wanted to savor these moments before meeting Pierre and consciously mark the transition. She wished to study everything here as she had done the mountains to be sure that she was alive. The best thing about love is sometimes the final yard.

. . .

As Colette sat down in the Café de Lyon, a group of young girls caught her eye. The five of them weren't looking at the sky and the freshly glittering white stars in the east or the half-moon trailing its silver train across the waves. They weren't looking at the black hills or the rocky crags that loomed jagged and dark above the sea like thickets of rosemary. They paid no attention to the fading light in the west, shot through with the last filaments of sundown, nor did they notice that the light was powdered with gold sparks and flecks of cherry red. It looked as if these unknown girls took in none of the world as it was despite all its best entreaties and its constant renewal.

Young girls are like delicate skiffs. They were so fearful and so greedy for life that every one of their hearts was ready to burst with the painful abundance.

But they couldn't see it. All they could see were their own supposed shortcomings, even though these things were inconsequential. You don't have to be perfect to be loved. Quite the opposite: You have to be you.

Colette thought she could make out tiny lights on the girls' bodies and faces. She finished her glass of rosé and strode off confidently into her new life. However long it might last, she was determined to pay attention to all the new experiences.

Pierre had cooked for her, and anyone watching would have seen a prayer in motion. They sat down at a table with lit candles on it, and he looked at her as if he couldn't possibly take in enough of this moment.

"We're living a miracle," he said.

"We are," Colette replied.

He raised her hand to his lips.

A spark.

. . .

On Vida's rest day a week after the salon, Édou picked her up at the hotel in his car.

"Time to think of yourself," he said. "Right now."

He knew that she loved looking after the hotel and its guests. He could tell that she got absorbed in her work and that it wouldn't be easy to create space inside her for doing nothing and feeling fine, even when she wasn't there. He had time, and he would make the most of that time until the day he died.

They drove out of the valley and over the four mountains, had a picnic in the cedar forest and a dip in the river, and then lazed around in the garden of his manor, stroking and hiding their heads as the pain that pain had prevented them from feeling gradually subsided.

Am I enough for you? their eyes said.

Help! their faces said.

It would take a while.

Love cannot do everything. Not immediately, in any case. But there does come a time when, yes, I can do anything.

On the eighth day after the Littéramour salon, Jean Finkielkraut invited Géraldine Châtelet for a coffee (two even, as people in the Boulangerie Raspail breathlessly reported) and then took her to Luc le Marseillais's *bar tabac* for an aperitif. They did a lot of laughing but called each other "monsieur" and "madame" throughout, as they prolonged their lunch in his garden far into the afternoon. After that, they barely stopped talking about books as they cooked and ate and drank and danced and argued and rowed and breathed and made up and so on. Any role they could play for each other. What a wild dance of the soul, what a sulfurous first night as they hurled themselves into lovemaking with such abandon that they forgot to be ashamed of their no-longer-so-youthful bodies.

"Whoever would have imagined it," Francis said one night at dinner. It was no longer possible just to turn up at Jean's house whenever he felt like it. He missed their impromptu meetings, but on the other hand . . .

He reached gently for Elsa's hand, which was no longer curled up into a fist next to her plate, and held it against his cheek. "I love you so much."

"I love you, Francis," she repeated again and again. She couldn't say it often enough to make up for twenty years of silence.

Marie-Jeanne quietly stepped out into the evening light. Where there was compassion, there was also comfort. And her comfort was like a fountain or a tabletop firework display. And yet she still felt the pain.

Falling in love is when two people can't stop looking at each other.

Being in love is when two people look in the same direction.

Being beyond love is when there is no one to look out for you.

. . .

One month after the salon, Valérie and Marie-Jeanne drove out to a cemetery in the mountains, one of those graveyards high up on a slope below one of the Drôme's many ruined villages. Simple metal crosses from the wars, and weathered gravestones from the century before last. Dense silence.

They sat for a long time on a gravestone bearing a picture of Valérie's best friend, the love of her life, a great romance involving separate bedrooms and not a single kiss.

"She's inside me, you know? Gabriela. Her voice and her scent, her jokes, her smile, and her way of thinking. Every time I feel myself yearning for her, I go for a walk inside myself and let the memories come and go. Every single one. And then I weep and I laugh and I miss her. And then I tell her that I will soon be there too."

"Soon? Are you trying to tell me something, Madame M.?"

" 'Soon' is entirely relative in the various hereafters. To be honest, I'd love to spend a few more decades loaning books and, who knows, organizing a few more salons where the focus is actually on literature."

She got to her feet.

"I always leave a poem here for her," Valérie said. "Actually, I leave one here for myself because only her name is here at the cemetery."

She closed her eyes, breathed in, opened her eyes again, and gazed at the picture on the headstone.

When you spoke
You were my half of the sky

When you slept
You were pure love and sea
When you died
I was your earth.

Six weeks after the salon, Marie-Jeanne saddled up her foam-white horse.

Marie-Jeanne Claudel's last conversation with the olive tree for now

Napoléonne was grazing around the tree, chewing the blades of grass she plucked from the soil. Marie-Jeanne lay in the shade, her face turned up to the branches, her feet resting against the trunk. The olive tree, which didn't like to give its age, delighted in the play of the light and the shadows of its leaves on this beloved face.

Her gaze was inscrutable and yet there was something in her gestures—the beginnings of a scar, an expression that would become more pronounced over time. It was the profound heartache of being naked and alone in life.

She told the tree everything, and it listened attentively to her. When she had presented her plan in full, it tried not to insist that she refrain from implementing it. That was another truth: Everyone has the right to pursue their own unhappiness, including Marie-Jeanne.

Her thirteen years were all she had. Youth, stupidity, recklessness, earnestness, and bravery. Everything was new. It was her first time for everything.

"By the way," Marie-Jeanne asked at the end, "one last

question: If I ever wanted to stop seeing the southern lights, how would that work?"

The tree told her. She hugged her friend and scratched its back one last time. The olive tree lowered its branches, its young shoots and soft twigs, as far as it judged possible to embrace the girl. It couldn't, though, because that was not in its nature. Why, oh why, didn't it rain that day?

33

Fifteen Years Later

Every year, always on the feast of St. Lawrence, Marie-Jeanne returned to Nyons. This was now the tenth time since she had turned eighteen. It had become a tradition for the wedded Loulou and Luca; the unwaveringly formal tango-dancing couple Géraldine and Jean; Marie-Jeanne's foster parents, Francis and Elsa; the mobile librarian Valérie Montesquieu; and Colette the calligrapher and her chef husband, Pierre, to all meet up at Vida and Édouard's La Dolce Vita hotel. They would gather in the library and eat, drink, and chat away until midnight before going out onto the terrace, throwing back their heads, and applying themselves to making wishes.

"Do you remember?" someone would say during dessert at the latest. "Do you remember how we almost didn't meet?"

"You enjoyed going to the cheese stall at the market a million times more than offering me a polite bonjour, my love. You really need to ask yourself what those cheeses had that I didn't."

Gallantly taking the retired solicitor's hand, Jean said, "It was winking at me, madame."

The two of them flashed ever-youthful glances at each other.

Loulou and Luca brought along their twin daughters, Marie and Jeanne. In the first couple of years, the girls slept in their wicker baskets, then they started crawling under the table, pulling people's trouser legs and the tablecloth, and later they turned into bookworms who worked their way through the shelves of Vida's library and told their adopted aunt (Loulou's title for Marie-Jeanne) about all the books they'd read.

The former bric-a-brac dealer Francis Meurienne's wife, Elsa, was now a famous local author of cookbooks that had been translated into several languages. Francis himself continued to deliver books on loan or for purchase to acquaintances of whom he had grown very fond. One such client was the Parisian who used to live in the long-defunct commune but had now become a farmer, no longer speaking in riddles but straight from the heart.

"Who's coming to Monsieur Mussigmann's Festival du Livre this year?" asked Pierre, who was, as usual, cooking for everyone.

Over the years, Francis had taken advantage of helping Monsieur Mussigmann with preparations for the literary festival in order to speak to the people whose books he read. His conclusion was that they were just like him. Although the Nyons town council had begun to build a library, the bookabus still crisscrossed the valleys and hills, though now there was an official partnership with the council and the *département* paid the librarians' salaries.

Valérie was still an adviser on which books to stock, and

every time she spoke about literature the glow would light up on her lips. Marie-Jeanne worried, though. The fifteen years had left their mark on her friend, who was now eighty-one and had been forced to swap her lace-trimmed parasol for a more solid walking stick.

Valérie called out the names—"Roald Dahl! Christine Dupont!"—and Colette held up her poster designs.

Marie-Jeanne was grateful to her extended family for never asking her any questions about why she had once more come unaccompanied and why they never heard her mention a significant other. Occasionally she wondered if Valérie might not have informed the rest of the group, but if she had, there wouldn't have been any of these conversations—"Remember how we might not have met if it hadn't been for the salon?"—that generally segued into speculation about all the fateful coincidences necessary for them all to meet up that one magical evening.

"Imagine if Francis had never come up with the idea of the bookabus."

"Just think if I'd never come to live here."

"Or just imagine if I'd never been born."

"Or if you'd stayed with that boring André."

"He wasn't really that boring."

"You dung beetle!"

"You monster!"

Valérie and Marie-Jeanne exchanged a discreet glance, looked down at their plates, and muttered something like "Really quite extraordinary" under their breath.

"How's the bookshop going?" Francis asked his daughter. Her face had changed over the past eighteen months. There were smile lines around her lips, and her eyes were a warm blue color, albeit veiled with delicate sadness.

"I still hold a literary salon every Wednesday and I'm going to rent a café and the bistro next door to have more space."

She didn't mention that the literary salon was extremely well attended. Word seemed to have spread. An incredible number of couples had met at Marie's Lumières du Sud bookshop over the past decade. This meant that the events she still called "Littéramour" after her very first book club for lonely hearts were not only packed with book lovers longing to hear Marie-Jeanne and her assistant Lili talk about authors and new publications or to listen to a writer reading their work. People of all ages also came along on the lookout for love. Sometimes they came alone, wearing their hearts on their sleeves, sometimes as a group of five—boisterous ladies' clubs, gangs of girls. And sometimes in twos: a man searching for love, and his best friend. There were more and more of them, which was another reason Marie-Jeanne was seeking to expand.

A bookshop and a carefully managed card index detailing the profiles of her customers (and their southern lights) had proved the perfect cover. Here and there she would drop an invitation in a specific letterbox before introducing the potential couple at the bookshop over a glass of wine and some stories and leaving the rest to the alchemy of books. Marie-Jeanne couldn't do any more than that—but she couldn't do any less either.

She spent her time reading, selling books, looking for southern lights, and then arranging for their owners to meet freely on paper wings. Her bookshop had become a magical place. It didn't take long for this to become an open secret, and more and more people would drive three or four hours to Lumières du Sud in the hope of finding more than just a good book.

"Will you invite me sometime, Mademoiselle Marie-Jeanne?" Jean asked. He had refashioned himself as a writer of romantic comedies and given up trying to please reviewers in far-off Paris. "I've returned to an old idea for a book. I only recently remembered it, and I've no idea why I didn't pursue it at the time. It was about a mobile library, books, love, and so on. Imagine this: Couples are connected long before they meet by a kind of invisible bond of light and—"

"What a ghastly idea!" Valérie squeaked.

"Terrible," Marie-Jeanne said. "It would never sell."

"I told you you were getting a bit odd in your old age, monsieur," Géraldine said, giving Jean a delicate peck on the cheek.

I sat quietly among them, as I always did. I liked what they had done with me and with what I had left them.

With the exception of Marie-Jeanne.

All those silent nights.

She looked out for everyone else, and no one looked out for her. Of course, she had friendships, some close, others not so close. A few men fell in love with her and others lusted after her, but she always found the right words to evade them. She tried kissing and found it extremely pleasurable, and yet she kept wondering what it would feel like to kiss someone you loved.

I watched Marie-Jeanne with her long, dark hair, which she always wore up, her blue eyes behind round black-framed glasses. Never any makeup. Her uncaressed body under her outfit of white shirt and jeans. The steady gaze with which she peered into the bottom of people's hearts with consideration and concern. Her strength, and the way she still appreciated the beauty in things.

Édou sat down at the piano. This part of the evening was also a long-standing tradition. Jean and Pierre knew the lyrics of many popular French tunes and chansons by heart—"La Mer," "La Vie en Rose," "Boum!," "Les Champs-Élysées"—and Madame Châtelet showed off her impressive jazz vocals for "Summertime" and "Lullaby of Birdland," whereupon Jean would glow with pride.

Colette shimmied so languidly and hypnotically to these songs that Pierre forgot to eat. Luca and Loulou swayed across the floor cheek to cheek, while the twins sat on either side of Valérie, their eyes shiny with tiredness.

Maybe it was the sum of all the years, the sum of evenings like this surrounded by loving couples, that made Marie-Jeanne get up and leave. It still hurt that no one looked at her with desire or pride in their eyes. She'd missed out on habits and tacit agreements built up over many years; she had no tally of imperfect and perfect years.

And so shortly before midnight, not long before the river of Perseids would appear and stars come streaming down from the sky on a night when any wish was permitted, she left.

Marie-Jeanne remembered what the olive tree had told her to do if and when she wanted to become blind to the wonders of love. To let go of me. Because that was what she had to do: She had to let go of me to take full advantage of me. She had to stop seeing and understanding me in order to lose herself in me.

That is why I was always present on the feast of St. Lawrence, and I respected Marie-Jeanne's decision. Everything is possible on the night of wishes. Her white shirt in the darkness. She fled so she wouldn't disturb the others and could become one with the night.

She walked up the mountain toward the Col Renard, where she could be close to the sky and watch the delicate threads of southern lights streaming upward.

I sat down beside her.

Starry teardrops—the Perseids were on their way.

"Are you there?" Marie-Jeanne said after some time.

"Yes, I'm here, Marie-Jeanne. I'm always with you."

"If you're there, then show yourself. I need to tell you something."

And since it was her, I showed myself. She didn't look directly at me. She kept staring up at the sky, but then she smiled.

"I always knew you looked like a man," she said, "but you represent all of everything, don't you?"

"Yes," I replied. It's true that my outward appearance is what humans think of as a man's. Not young, not old, dark hair with a few strands of gray, a face that could as easily belong to a woman as to a man, and not too beautiful. Love is never just beautiful.

"Leave me," Marie-Jeanne said, "and then come back." Now she turned to look at me, her expression calm and resolute.

She waited. We both waited. We needed an ally, just one, and not long afterward a star sacrificed itself for us. The shooting star blazed slowly across the firmament, green and golden.

"My wish is that I should leave you. My wish is to be

blinded by love. My wish is not to know love. My wish is that I should know nothing of you."

The shooting star paled to nothing.

"I love you," I said to Marie-Jeanne.

Then she looked at me, and I realized she hadn't heard me. I raised my hand and caressed her cheek, her mouth, her eyelids, her heart, and her hands. Her arms and her neck and her knees. I touched her everywhere and felt intoxicated. I wrapped her in everything I had while she stared out at the southern lights, and eventually her eyebrows puckered. She was searching.

Now she saw the world as every other human being did: in shades of affection, desire, and love, with the feeling that she had arrived. A mystery as impenetrable as the wide, open spaces of the night.

"You're gone," she whispered. She buried her face in her hands and wept the tears of a lonely person weeping with guilt and relief, shame and gratitude, and it broke my stupid, thoughtless heart.

"Marie-Jeanne!" Vida called from the terrace. "It's starting. The shooting stars are on their way!"

Marie-Jeanne made her way back as if her body were a house on fire. I could see her knees trembling, her heart beating at a different rate, the pain sneaking into her body. Pain, longing, and a tugging: There she went, a woman in love. And now came the despair—whom did she love? who loved her?—and it pounced on her like a predator.

Yet she was smiling through her tears. She hugged them all, one after the other.

"What's wrong, my love?" Elsa asked, wiping away her daughter's tears.

"Are you having a hard time at the bookshop?" Francis asked.

She shook her head, and now it was visible only to me: The southern light illuminating her entire body floated up—no, hurled itself!—into the night air and became longer and longer.

Her prince was already born. He was already looking for her. I had chosen him many years earlier, before I even suspected that she would let go of me. I was incapable of telling her whether he would ever find her or when, and what she would make of the opportunity was equally uncertain. I could bribe Fate and Chance, Wonder and Time, but they all had their own ruthless intentions.

It might happen the next day or only fifty years from now. It might happen on any day and at any time, without warning or preceding omen, just when she least expected it. I strike people in the midst of their daily lives. I come, I stay, I leave. Just like that, and there's nothing any of you can do about it. Nothing at all.

34

Who Knows What They Love and What They Hate, What They Want and Where They Belong, When They Don't Have Books?

"You're sure you can cope?" Lili asked, pointing to the twelve boxes of books. Her attitude suggested that she was afraid her boss might say: "Actually, I'm not."

"Of course I'll cope. Go off and meet your Marc-Antoine."

"He's not *my* Marc-Antoine!"

"You sure?"

Lili blushed, mumbled something like, "We're just going out for an ice cream," and shut the shop door behind her. In all her blushing, Marie-Jeanne's assistant forgot to turn the sign from *Open* to *Closed*.

Marie-Jeanne set about unpacking the next load of books. They had ordered new publications and sent back unsold stock in preparation for the next salon and for the Easter holiday weekend. She took a pile of her fresh purchases and climbed the ladder.

She loved these evenings in Lumières du Sud after closing time, just her and the books with some music playing quietly in the background. A dialogue with lots of different fictional characters as she immersed herself in her ocean of stories.

Standing on the ladder, she rearranged the shelf order. The years 1985 and 1986 had produced a profusion of crime novels, confessional fiction, and political nonfiction, as well as wide-ranging fantasy books.

"Oh, hello there, Mr. Updike," she said as she came to the top shelf. "Mind budging over a little bit?"

She removed and rearranged things, rediscovered a few gems and moved them one shelf lower down. That one should go on display next to the register, she should really read this one again, and . . .

The bell on the inside of the door gave a discreet tinkle.

"Bonsoir, madame. I know I'm much too late, but I couldn't ignore you. Your bookshop, I mean. Sorry, I'm talking gibberish. How about I come inside and make an effort not to stammer like an idiot?"

Marie-Jeanne didn't immediately turn around and look down to see the source of the unfamiliar voice. A man. She could hear the smile in his words. Warmth. Calm. Stars. And a nervousness that surprised the speaker.

She adjusted the books until they were perfectly aligned, even though they had already been as neatly arrayed as soldiers on parade. She ran her fingers over the names on the spines. Sten Nadolny, Marion Zimmer Bradley, John Updike, Douglas Adams, Alice Walker . . .

Any day, any time. At the very moment you least expected it, suddenly, something began to glow.

She wanted to give herself a little time to note the exact moment and how it began. Because the strange, unprecedented ache under her heart was telling her that something was now beginning. Her whole inner world was expanding and brightening. Not to mention the incomparable sense of joy! It was nothing like the joy she felt when she picked out a new book by one of her favorite authors from a fresh delivery. Nothing like the irrepressible awesomeness of accelerating her old Triumph motorbike through one of the region's tunnels. Or going back to Nyons and letting the twins Jeanne and Marie jump around on their adoptive aunt's tummy as if she were a human trampoline and listen wide-eyed to her inexhaustible treasure chest of stories.

This joy came surging up inside her like a sweet, life-giving earthquake. So this was what it felt like? It was the greatest sensation on earth.

Any second now, she would turn around and gaze into the eyes that loved her. Any moment now, she and the stranger would see each other. He would be beautiful, whether he was handsome or not, however old he was. It would be painful and joyful living with him. They would love each other. For one night? For a year? Maybe forever.

Marie-Jeanne smiled to herself and turned to face him. "Stay," she said. "I've been waiting for you."

The man looked up at her with his blue eyes from under dark hair as if unsurprised by her response. Unsurprised, charmed, and irritated, all at once. He smiled and stretched out his hand to help her down from the ladder.

This unknown, foaming white light inside her glowed ever more brightly, and she took his hand. They stood there, silently smiling, shy, familiar and yet foreign.

It was beginning.

One Last Conversation

"Don't you miss it just a little bit?" asked the olive tree, which didn't talk about its age.

"What am I supposed to be missing? Fate snapping its jaws? Chance sitting around out of work? Logic acting all snooty? Do you know how many lovers suddenly identified each other—click!—and took a shortcut via Chaos?"

"Yes. Four thousand one hundred and eight."

"That's half the population of a small town."

"Or a large village. Now what?" the olive tree asked. "What do we do now?"

"Same as always—we watch and see what they make of it," I answered.

The tree rustled its leaves lugubriously. "What do you think—will someone write about all of this one day?"

"Who would do it?" I asked.

"Maybe a magic-weaver who uses extravagant words to write her way into a mountain man's life. She'll write a short, sweet story about the different kinds of love. Just for him. To console a single person."

"Why not?" I replied. "Books are the last alchemy of our age. They make anything possible. Anything."

The tree exhaled and stretched its limbs, and I leaned back against its proud, ancient trunk, and it felt good to be Love. I'm not perfect. I generally arrive at inconvenient moments. But I help you to live and I help you to die. I am all of everything.

Postface

A book called *Southern Lights* first appeared in my novel *The Little Paris Bookshop*. It existed as an entirely fictitious book within a work of fiction, written by the pseudonymous Sanary.

"Sanary's *Southern Lights* was the only thing that pierced him without hurting him. Reading *Southern Lights* was a homeopathic dose of happiness. It was the only balm that could ease Perdu's pain—a gentle cold stream over the scorched earth of his soul."

This extract comes at the beginning of the story, when we first get to know the Parisian bookseller Jean Perdu and his Literary Apothecary—a floating bookshop on a converted barge from which Perdu sells books as medicine and otherwise tries to avoid feeling any emotion. That is because emotion equals love, and love equates to missing Manon.

As I wrote then, *Southern Lights* was a story about the various kinds of love, "full of wonderful invented words and infused with an enormous humanity." Thinking of the book, "all he could see was light sparkling on a river. 'That book is like the woman I used to love. It leads to her. It's liquid love.

It's the dose I could more or less bear and yet nevertheless feel. It's the straw I've been breathing through for the last twenty years.' "

He had no luck finding out who Sanary was, however: " 'Sanary'—named after the erstwhile town of refuge for exiled writers, Sanary-sur-Mer on the south coast of Provence—was an impenetrable pseudonym. His—or her—publisher, Duprés, was in an old people's home out in Île-de-France enduring Alzheimer's with good cheer. During Perdu's visits, the elderly Duprés had served him up a couple of dozen versions of who Sanary was and how the manuscript had come into his possession."

The bookseller has been searching for the person behind the pen name for twenty years, and *The Little Paris Bookshop* describes Perdu's odyssey, accompanied by Max, Cuneo, and a whole retinue of lovable characters, to discover the author's identity.

The person behind the pseudonym is finally unmasked in the final third of the novel—but I'm not going to spoil it for you here. I will reveal this much, however: The author is indeed a woman. She wrote *Southern Lights* in the late eighties so that someone would come looking for her. Someone would eventually love her as if she were the very bedrock of his existence.

Following the publication of *The Little Paris Bookshop* in German in 2013 and its subsequent translation into thirty-seven languages, I received hundreds of letters from readers in Warsaw and São Paulo, Athens and Ohio, inquiring about *Southern Lights,* and each time I had to admit that it was a fictitious book within my novel. As is *The Night* by Max Jordan (whom I miss terribly—I'd really love to know what became of him, and of Jean Perdu and his boat. One by one, the sequels to *The Little Paris Bookshop* will be written).

"There are books that were written for one person only," Perdu says.

I promised my readers that I would turn the fictitious *Southern Lights* into a real novel—a book about the various kinds of love, told as if it were written for a single human being.

I have kept my promise.

Acknowledgments

I know absolutely nothing about love, and the older I get, the less I understand it.

That is what I said one day to my husband, Jens Johannes Kramer, and his reply was: "But that's the way it must be if you want to lose yourself in love."

He therefore deserves to be the first recipient of my gratitude, because his words kept whispering away inside me until after many years I thought: *That is what I want to write about now*. Our incomprehension of love and the fact that if we think we understand it, then we cannot possibly be in love.

Jens, you are my best friend, you are my family and my writing partner and my husband. Thank you for being exactly as you are. By the way, I have no idea why I love you and you love me, which strikes me as a positive state of affairs.

Anja Keil has been my agent for almost fifteen years now. Thanks for your suggestion to replace jazz with a chanson. Thanks too to Doris Janhsen, Natalja Schmidt, and Steffen

Haselbach for forming a unique and illuminating editing trio.

Of course, a writer is never alone when a book is brought into the world—and especially when the world is on the other side of the Atlantic. My special thanks therefore go to the great Cecile Barendsma, Keil & Keil's co-agent in New York City, as my literary accomplice. And to the translator, Simon Pare: His craft makes all my manuscripts shine.

I would also like to thank the whole team at Ballantine Books for their passion, accuracy, and editorial courage, in particular Hilary Rubin Teeman, executive editor; Caroline Weishuhn, assistant editor; the publishers, Kim Hovey, Jennifer Hershey, and Kara Welsh; the best publicity and marketing team ever, Chelsea Woodward, Taylor Noel, and Megan Whalen; and those who gave the text a touchable gestalt from the production team, Pamela Alders and Luke Epplin.

Un grand merci also to Benoît and Caro and to Violetta. I was able to sleep and write and observe in the *mazet* La Traversière in Condorcet and in Violetta's hotel La Dolce Vita, both of which can be found on www.abritel.fr.

The Nyons bookseller Monsieur Mussigmann has yet to discover his good fortune at being teleported back to the period between 1968 and 1986. Do go and experience his biennial literary festival for yourselves; it's such a magnificently mad idea. Also, there was in fact a mobile library in Nyons until its demise in the midnineties.

My affectionate gratitude also goes out to my test readers Janet Clark, Catrin George Ponciano, Carlos Collado Seidel, Christian Mees, Angela Schwarz, and Leon Sachs. You will find your favorite opening in the workshop fragments, and you know the jazz version.

. . .

Last but not least, I would like to thank Love. Let me tell you this, you awful pest—I still don't understand you, but I'm grateful to you for being you, for all the yearning and tugging, the missing and kissing and non-kissing. For the hugs when we least expect them. For the tears and the turmoil and the peace that comes afterward.

I've been happy, so I know how it feels.

And I shall not be a love coward—I shall always love.

Nina George, June 2019

About the Author

Nina George is the author of *The Little Paris Bookshop, The Little French Bistro,* and *The Book of Dreams. The Little Paris Bookshop* spent more than forty weeks on the *New York Times* bestseller list and was translated into thirty-six languages. George is president of the European Writers' Council. She is married to the writer Jens J. Kramer, and together they also write mystery novels and children's books. Nina George lives in Berlin and in a little fishing village in the Brittany.

ninageorge.de
nina-george.com

About the Type

This book was set in Bembo, a typeface based on an old-style Roman face that was used for Cardinal Pietro Bembo's tract *De Aetna* in 1495. Bembo was cut by Francesco Griffo (1450–1518) in the early sixteenth century for Italian Renaissance printer and publisher Aldus Manutius (1449–1515). The Lanston Monotype Company of Philadelphia brought the well-proportioned letterforms of Bembo to the United States in the 1930s.